The World Beneath Trilogy

Rebecka Lynn

Table of Contents:

The Magical Violin – Pg. 5

The Petrified Kingdom of the Gourges – Pg. 67

The Pirates of the Unknown Sea- Pg. 181

The Magical Violin

Book 1

CHAPTER 1

The young man continued walking through the woods listening to the ground crunching as he went on. It was a beautiful forest mixed with hemlock fir and various types of evergreen needleleaf trees. There was a soft breeze blowing and ahead of him was the cottage. The cottage had been a birthday gift for him when he had turned eight. The cottage was a project between his grandfather and father. It was used as a clubhouse or to get away at times when the boy had things on his mind or even to get some peace. Today the boy was in desperate need to getaway. Earlier that day he had attended his grandfather's funeral who he had a close bond with. His grandfather had fought in a war, and during that time, he brought home a wooden violin. When Gordon returned home from the war, he gifted the violin to his son and hoped that he would play it. Years passed, and the violin was passed on to Edwin.

"You'll never find another violin like it," said Gordan in a memory Edwin thought of while he began to light a fire in the fireplace near an old couch in the cottage.

"Once upon a time a long, long time ago, some hallow tree seeds had been lost all around the universe. They were scattered to millions of different places, and no one knows where all of them landed. Someone made a big mess!" said Gordon. "What's a hal-

low tree?" asked Edwin. "Hallow trees are magical trees which were used to create secret passageways. They are giant trees with yellow fruit and white trunks, and when they grow to be a considerable size, a hole appears at their roots which becomes the doorway to another place." Edwin then started to play the old violin as he continued thinking back on the strange childhood stories his grandfather had told him.

THE SYCAMORE TREE

The soldier was exhausted. He stopped near a stream and stuck his face into the water, not worrying about whether it was safe or not. He just wanted to quench his thirst and didn't care if he got sick later. As he was bathing, he then began to hear something strange. He started to hear voices coming from what looked like a sycamore tree. The soldier finished his bath and went towards the tree. "Hmm' he thought. It was a strange type of sycamore tree. At the roots of the tree, he noticed a large hole which he could fit into and he also saw that the tree was enormous, too big to be a sycamore tree. The voices began again, and the soldier decided to explore the hole inside the tree. When the soldier finally got to the end of the tunnel underneath the sycamore tree (or at least he thought it was a sycamore tree), he stepped out inside some kind

of building that looked like a laboratory, and as he looked up, he saw a woman in front of him. "Hello," said the woman. "I mean you no harm," she said.

SPINNING

The room began to spin, and there was nothing Edwin could do to stop it. He didn't realize that the song that he played on the violin was a key to open a doorway into another place. Lights of many colors encircled around him, and it was as though he was being pulled through a never-ending water slide. As he went through the tunnel, he passed by what looked like glimmering stars and planets and other galaxies. Finally, he went through a blinding cloud of light which hurt his eyes and arrived at some other place. There was a cold, wet substance beneath him which resembled snow, but it was blue and glowed, and it reminded him of cotton candy. The sky in this other place was dark, and there were no stars, but there was some light in the heavens. The light in the skies was green and looked like the Aurora Borealis. "Wow," he thought.

THE GREAT ESCAPE

"Ten seconds to launching," said Luna, the ship's automated voice. "Beginning count down now... ten" "Hurry, Meagles!" cried Lady Inera. "Hurry!

Velaticcus will soon find out," she said. "Nine...eight...seven..." "Did you get the seeds? He'll find us if you didn't and I hope you took them all" "six...five...four...three... "Yes, I got them all; we should be fine," said Meagles, "two...one... blast off! Away they went, Meagles (an attendant) and Lady Inera just launched themselves away in an escape pod off-planet Ahirine.

Meagles had been rescued by Lady Inera's father when she was an infant.

He had come from the planet Vonkernera to Ahirine seeking asylum since his planet had been conquered by Velaticcus when Lady Inera had just been born. Vonkernera was a purplish-green planet about the size of our Saturn, but it did not have rings, and it had four moons. The moons were used to keep track of the different seasons, when the seasons changed, the moons above also changed. There were once vibrant blue seas that glimmered and various types of wonderful forests which existed nowhere else. Vonkernera was inhabited by a unique race of creatures who called themselves Vonkerns.

Vonkerns were froglike creatures that walked upright like humans, who were tall, and their skin was blue and silver or red and silver in color with large blue oval eyes. As lady Inera and Meagles escaped from Ahirine, Meagles sadly reflected on the destruction of his own planet. "We shouldn't have trusted him" wallowed Lady Inera as she now felt the deep loss of her father. "I knew we couldn't trust him," she sobbed. Lady Inera was the recent captured prize of a lusting War Lord, Velaticcus. Velaticcus was a tyrant. He was the ruler of the planet Zenkov, and he had just conquered Lady Inera's planet and had begun to enslave her people. Lady Inera's father and Velaticcus had just made a truce, but unfortunately Velaticcus poisoned Lady Inera's father when he was rejected as a suitor for Lady Inera.

Velaticcus had asked Heronis, (Lady Inera's father) for permission to have Lady Inera's hand in marriage in hopes that in marrying her he could also rule over Ahirine, but Heronis refused to give his daughter to such a tyrant.

LOST PRIZE

"Where is she!' bellowed Velaticcus. "I...I... don't know," said his best warrior. "How did she escape," said Velaticcus as he now lifted Kronogar by his neck and looking him in the eye pinning him against the wall.

"Find her and bring her back to me," growled the angry tyrant. "Yes" whimpered Kronogar as Velaticcus dropped him on the ground. "We can't let her get away," said Velaticcus.

What had happened a long time ago before Lady Inera had been born, Heronis had a team a weapon engineers create a weapon that could destroy an entire planet. When the weapon had been completed, he hid it in another world which was unknown to Velaticcus. Heronis created this weapon after he had seen what Velaticcus had done to Vonkernera. When Lady Inera grew up, her father told her about the weapon and where it was located, in case there ever came a time for when she needed to use it.

LOST IN SPACE

Meagles and Lady Inera had been drifting in space for some time now. They had been in such a hurry to escape that they had not planned what to do or where to go once they escaped. "How much food do we have?" Asked Lady Inera.

The pod they were in was large enough for at least five people and had been stocked with enough food to last five people for at least six months, but a Vonkern needed twice as much food as a human.

It was a cozy type of spacecraft where someone could survive quite comfortably, and there were even games similar to; our board games like monopoly that one could play while traveling or exploring through space. "Let's go to the lab," said Meagles. "I bet that's where your father hid the map to the weapon." He said. "Good idea," said Lady Inera.

TRAITOR

Out he went into the pod at the speed of lightning. Kronogar was on his way back to Zenkov. His plan had worked, he had given Meagles the keys to where the escape pods were located so he could take Lady Inera and flee to the secret lab where Heronis's team of scientists lived. Kronogar was actually, a traitor and a spy. He betrayed Velaticcus after the capture of Vonkernera when his own family had been enslaved in the process. After Velaticcus had made a truce with Heronis, Heronis made Kronogar promise that he would look after his daughter. For years Heronis and Kronogar had met secretly from time to time, and Kronogar tried talking Heronis out of making a truce with Velaticcus, but Heronis was desperate for peace and so decided to take his chances. Now, Kronogar was heading back to meet with others who were not loyal to Velaticcus to make plans on how to overthrow him.

ENNIAD

Enniad was a teeny; tiny planet which looked more like a moon, and it even circled around a larger gas planet which could never sustain life. Some astronauts from Ahirine had accidentally come across it when they were on their way back home after months of exploring areas in space where no one had ever ventured.

The astronauts had to do an emergency landing when a part of the craft had been damaged in an unexpected meteor shower and randomly picked Enniad to land on. After landing, they realized that it was going to take some time to fix the craft and so the astronauts decided to explore the new area until they were ready to return home. They discovered that life could be sustained on Enniad with a little terraforming and decided to create a lab. As time passed and much of the planet was terraformed, a strange and unique form of tree began to grow. The trees looked like giant sycamore trees, but after much experimentation with the trees, the scientists discovered that if the trees grew in the soil of certain places besides its native soil it would hallow out at the roots and you could go through the holes and come up in the place where the soil came from. In discovering this, the scientists decided to safeguard some of the seeds of the trees and sent some back to Heronis. Later, after the capture of Vonkernera, Enniad was used as a haven for some of the Vonkerns who were able to escape the enslavement of their planet.

CHAPTER 2

"Who are you?" asked the soldier. "You may call me Lady Inera," said the woman. She was a tall woman with hair past her waist, and she was wearing a long laced hooded cloak that was silver in color. "And...who are you?" asked Lady Inera. "I am Private Gordan, said the bewildered soldier.

What had occurred was that during the war, which Gordan was part of, he somehow got separated from his unit during an ambush and had been wandering for some time in the woods trying to find fellow soldiers.

"A soldier?" she asked. "Yes, I am a soldier" "Hmm, she said, it seems my father made an interesting discovery" "I'm not understanding ...and uh...what are you doing here" questioned the bewildered soldier. He was wondering what such a lovely woman was doing alone in a strange lab underground in the woods during a bloody war. He didn't realize that he had entered Enniad. What had happened was that when Lady Inera and Meagles finally arrived to Enniad, Inera discovered a tree that had been quarantined away from the rest of the hallow trees and it had been growing in some dirt that had been planted in some extraterrestrial soil from a newly discovered planet. That newly discovered planet was Earth. The scientists took some of our Earths' soil back to Enniad and planted a seed from a hallow tree in it which then created a portal from Enniad to Earth. "Come with me," said Inera. She grabbed Gordan's arm and began walking back to the pod.

BETRAYED

"Any word of Kronogar?" asked Velaticcus. "No, said Armant." Armant was a warrior of Zenkov. He had been jealous of Kronogar for much time and desired to replace him. Kronogar was Velaticcus's most trusted warrior. He had joined the Service of Zenkov when he was a child and was extremely loyal to Velaticcus up until his family was enslaved.

THE MAP

"It's got to be here somewhere," said Meagles. Lady Inera and Gordan had finally arrived at the pod. "Ahh!" screamed Gordon" When he saw Meagles. Gordon now thought he had been abducted by aliens.

He was about to turn and run out of the pod until Lady Inera lifted her hand, pointed it at the door, and made a fist.

When she made a fist, the door slammed shut! The race of humans that had evolved on Heronis had evolved on their planet millions of years before dinosaurs began to walk on our planet. Humans from Heronis possessed superhuman like powers but could not fly or breathe underwater; instead, they were capable of doing things you would imagine that a witch or a magician could do. "You're on another planet, and you have arrived during a galactic war," explained Inera. "My world has been taken over by a tyrant who is looking for me, and the creature that startled you is a Vonkern, he is helping me find a weapon that my father has hidden somewhere on this planet or in yours," said Inera. "I mean you no harm; you can go back through the portal where you entered, or you can stay and help us, but I strongly ask that you help us for when this tyrant discovers that there is yet another planet with advanced life, he will also try to conquer it." "Well, that's a tough question," said Gordan rather sarcastically trying to digest what he just heard. "I guess I'll stay here and fight in this war instead," said Gordan. "And...uh what does this weapon do?' ask Gordan. "It will kill Velaticcus, the tyrant who is enslaving my people,' said Inera. "Lady Inera" interrupted Meagles. "I think we have found it." Meagles had flipped on a switch on the master board of the pod where locations were calculated on a map, and a light appeared in the direction of earth through the portal. "Oh good," said Lady Inera, let's take the trackers and go. The three then headed back where Gordan had entered Enniad.

TIME TRAVEL

Now, to clear things up a bit, in the beginning of the story when Edwin played the tune on the violin that his father had given him, he didn't know that the waterslide like tunnel which he traveled through not only pulled him into a different world, but it also sucked him through time. He was taken back to the time when his grandfather was still alive and into a world which unknown to Lady Inera was created by her father on Earth. After the scientists from Ahirine had created the portal from Enniad to Earth, they would go in and out of the portal from the Lab and explore Earth. One of the scientists (who was a Vonkern in fact) had retrieved soil from his destroyed planet and planted a hallow tree seed inside a massive cave on Earth in it in hopes of recreating Vonkernera on Earth hidden away from Velaticcus. A portal successfully formed at the roots of the hallow tree planted inside the cave and on the other side, a world like the old Vonkernera formed. It was a world hidden within a world deep in the ground beneath an undiscovered cave on Earth.

VELATICCUS

Velaticcus, the tyrant, was a giant human-like creature. Although he much resembled a man, he was not. Zenkovians (aliens from Zenkov) were taller and much more physically stronger than the people from Ahirine; they had red skin with scales like an alligator, and their eyes were usually green or black, and their pupils could not be seen. Zenkovians were selfish creatures. They had used up all the resources on their own planet, and so now they would travel through space, conquering weaker planets and enslave them forcing them to join their military or provide Zenkov with resources.

THE PLAN

"We need to steal the fighter pods and meet Inera at the lab; by then, she will have the weapon." Said Kronogar, who finally met with the others in a hidden cave found in some mountains on Zenkov who wanted to overthrow Velaticcus. When we are there, we can make plans on how to destroy the main colony. When Velaticcus had been conquering planets, he would build military posts and colonies on the planets to rule over them and populate them with Zenkovians. Many of the enslaved female captives were forced into marrying Zenkov warriors, and a few were chosen to become part of Velaticcus's personal collection of wives. Kronogar then handed some keys to a Zenkovian, which unlocked the door to where the fighter pods were located. "I'll stay here and set up the false attack and report back to Velaticcus before he wonders why I've been gone for so long. Then I'll set him off course and meet you guys back at the lab," said Kronogar. "I know Armant is probably looking for me," he said. The group then agreed and went off on their assigned tasks.

HUNGRY

"I'm so hungry," thought Edwin. He had been wandering around the strange world for some time now. Then suddenly, there appeared before him a strange-looking rabbit. The rabbit had webbed feet and was eating what looked like some kind of fish. He then decided he would try to capture the strange rabbit, so he could eat it. Edwin took his sweater off and tried to sneak up on the rabbit and throw his sweater on it but missed! Off ran the rabbit and Edwin chased after it. It led him into a swamp and disappeared into some water. "Interesting," thought Edwin as he was walking around the swamp trying to find the weird rabbit. Suddenly, he heard some voices from a distance and saw the oddest thing in all his life. It was Meagles. "I found it!" Shouted Meagles. "Oh...my... God!" gasped Edwin as he gawked in horror at Meagles. "Edwin then fainted as the sight of Meagles shocked him! What had happened was that when Edwin was sucked back in time through the space tunnel, he landed inside the world that the Vonkern (who had been part of Heronis's team of scientists) had tried to recreate from Enniad. Gordan, Meagles and Lady Inera took Edwin and his violin back to the lab. The violin that Edwin had was something that the Heronis's team of scientists had created from a Hallow tree. "Well, this is strange," said Lady Inera. "How is this a weapon?" she asked. "Look what it does," said Gordon. Gordan then began to play a certain tune on it, and one of the walls in the lab began to crack. "Stop doing that!" exclaimed Meagles. "I bet it will destroy Velaticcus's colony," said Lady Inera.

KRONOGAR RETURNS

"Where have you been?' bellowed Velaticcus as he looked at Kronogar who had finally returned. "Did you find Lady Inera?" "No, Master," said Kronogar. "But I believe I found something else," he said. "What is it?' asked Velaticcus.

Meanwhile, while Kronogar was distracting Velaticcus, Armant had been secretly tracking Kronogar's traveling's. He wanted to prove once and for all that Kronogar was a traitor, so he could take his position. "This must be where the traitors meet," said Armant. He had arrived at the cave where Kronogar had gone earlier. "Let's destroy it and tell Velaticcus," said Armant to another warrior. "And go check on the fighter pods," he said to another warrior, but it was too late. The Zenkovian named Micco who Kronogar had given the keys to earlier to get the fighter pods had already stolen one of the ships and had freed some of the freshly enslaved

Ahirines that had been captured by Velaticcus after he killed Heronis.

Boom! The main ship which Kronogar and Velaticcus was in was hit by a fighter pod. "How did this happen?' yelled Velaticcus.

AWAKE

Edwin finally awoke. He sat up on top of the table where Meagles had placed him, and he looked around. "Here, eat this," said Gordan as he handed Edwin some food. "Who are you?" asked Edwin. "My name is Gordon." "That can't be!" exclaimed Edwin now recognizing his much younger grandfather. "You...you...died," he said. "I must be dreaming, or...did...I...die?" asked Edwin. "I think you bashed your head a bit," said Gordan. "No, no...you're my grandfather,' said Edwin. "See" Edwin then took a photograph out of his back-pant pocket and handed it to Gordan. "How can this be?" asked Gordon in a near whisper as he looked at the photograph. "It's the thing the boy was carrying," said Meagles. "Ahh!" screamed Edwin as he saw Meagles again. "He means you no harm," said Gordan. "I don't believe in aliens!" screamed Edwin. "Wake up!" screamed Edwin as he now began to slap himself on the face. "Wake up!" As soon as he was going to smack himself again. Lady Inera came into the lab and caught his hand. "You're not dead," she said. "You're on another planet and a weapon that my father created, which is also some kind of traveling-machine has brought you here."

TRICKED

"Ahhhh!" screamed Velaticcus as Kronogar pushed him out of the pod! "You traitor!" he yelled. Out went Kronogar. When the main ship had been attacked, Kronogar led Velaticcus into an escape pod taking him to the furthest part of the planet away from any civilization into a thick jungle infested with all kinds of unknown creatures and threw him out. Down went Velaticcus hitting several trees which knocked a few of his teeth out and landed on the ground with a hard thump. "Enjoy!" said Kronogar with a laugh as he shut the door to the pod and began to head to Enniad. "He's going to get it!" moaned Velaticcus to himself as he passed out on the ground bleeding. "Errrr," he moaned.

TREASON

"What happened?" snarled Armant when he finally arrived at the damaged main ship. "Someone stole the fighter pods and attacked us," said a warrior. "We've already begun repairs." He said. "Good." Said Armant, "And where is Velaticcus?" "Kronogar evacuated him," said the warrior. "Find him." Said Armant. "I am charging him with treason, and ready one of the cruiser ships for me, so I can find Lady Inera." He said.

MADE IT

"He's here." Said Meagles. "Huh?" Asked Lady Inera. "Kronogar," said Meagles. "He made it!" She exclaimed as Kronogar's pod landed. "More are on their way." Said Kronogar as he walked towards the lab. "Did you find the weapon?" He asked. "I'm not sure." Said Meagles. "But we found something," he said, pointing, to the violin. "That's it!" Said Kronogar. "We don't understand it," said Meagles. "We need to go back to Heronis; there's a piece missing and ...uh... who are they?' asked Kronogar now looking at Edwin and Gordan.

"They're beings from an intelligent civilization that my father's team discovered on another planet, the planet where he had put the weapon." Said Lady Inera. "Interesting," said Kronogar. "How did you get this asked Lady Inera to Edwin "My grandfather gave it to me." "That's not possible, this is the first time I've seen this weapon," said Gordon. "You're his grandfather?" asked Kronogar. "He traveled through time," said Gordon "Can we all stop explaining things, we don't have time to figure out who is who we need to figure out how this thing works," said Meagles. "Edwin, how did you get where we found you?' asked Lady Inera, "I played the song that my grandfather taught me," said Edwin. "A song?" asked Kronogar. "It must be a certain frequency," said Meagles. "Ahhh, yes, that makes sense now said Meagles. "I get it. Your grandfather made the weapon from the wood of a hallow tree, which is why when Edwin played the weapon, he was able to travel to our time" "That's weird," said Edwin. "How is that possible?" asked Lady Inera. "I don't know, but your father's scientists were geniuses," said Meagles. "They were here since you were an infant," said Meagles. "They had all the time in the world to experiment and explore without any outside interference," he said.

"Okay, everyone," said Kronogar, let's all hold on to each other, I'll hold onto Edwin and Edwin; you play the tune that your grandfather taught you." The group all held hands, and as Edwin played the violin, they all suddenly got sucked into the space tunnel that Edwin had gone through earlier, and they were all sent back to the place where Edwin had ended up in the first place. "You guys," said Kronogar "I don't think that it's a weapon, I think it was just a way for us to travel here, he must have hidden the weapon on Edwin's planet.

"This isn't my planet," said Edwin. "Wait!" said Meagles. "This is my planet; well sort of," he said. "Look! Let's follow the tracker," he said, pointing at a device on his arm which suddenly turned on its own which was some kind of map made out of advanced technology. "One of the scientists was a Vonkern after all," said Meagles. As they all followed the tracking device, it led them back through the other end of the hole where he had first entered the sycamore tree. "Well, this is strange," said Gordan. "Where's Edwin," asked Lady Inera, "Over here," said a voice. Edwin had now become invisible, and it was because when he followed the others through the hallow tree to his grandfather's time, he wasn't even born yet. "Wow," said Meagles.

BACK IN SPACE

"Lose them!" said Micco. While Kronogar, Meagles and everyone who had been at the lab were now on Earth, Micco, the rebel Zenkovian, who had damaged Velaticcus's main ship were being chased by Velaticcus's warriors, and he was trying to lose them. With him, were the other rebels who had met Kronogar in the cave on Zenkov. "We're never going to get to the lab," said one of the rebel warriors.

"Yes, we will," said Micco; we just have to lose them!" he cried.

HOPELESS

He felt *hopeless*. Velaticcus was still lying on the ground face down on planet Zenkov staring across at his teeth which had been knocked out. His legs were broken, and there was nothing he could do. "I can't believe I'm going to die here," he thought to himself.

"I guess I deserve this" he mumbled to himself as he shut his eyes trying to think of better times. Then, unexpectedly, there was a low growl which he heard coming from the direction where his feet were lying." Oh, no." He thought. He then began to try and crawl. As much as it hurt him to move, Velaticcus began to low crawl as fast as he could. A creature much like our tigers on earth was heading towards him. "Ahhh!" He cried like a helpless child. Right when the creature was about to bite his head, a giant rod came down on the animal and hit its nose, sending it whimpering away like a frightened dog.

Then, the rod hit Velaticcus's head, knocking him unconscious and whatever or whoever knocked him out began to drag him through the dark jungles of Zenkov.

EXPLORING

"This is fun!" said Edwin. "Now I'm like a superhero." He said. "Don't get too comfortable." Said Gordon. "So, where to now?" Asked Lady Inera. "East." Said Meagles. "I must warn you; there is also a war going on." Said Gordon. "What a coincidence." Said

Kronogar. The group continued walking for what seemed like days until finally they came to what looked like some mounds. "This looks like a good supply point." Said Gordon.

"What's that?" Asked Meagles.

"Where they keep weapons and explosives," Gordan replied. "Interesting." Said Meagles. "The tracker is leading us to that mound." He said, pointing to the left.

"Hmmm." Said Gordon. "I wonder." He thought. "Meagles how about you and Edwin go inside the mound and get what the tracker is taking you to? The rest of us will stay out here and keep a lookout in case anyone comes".

"Okay," said Meagles. "I have a better idea," said Edwin. "I'll just go by myself with the tracker," he said. Edwin then took the tracker from Meagles and went inside the mound. It led him to a large round bomb.

HIT

"We're hit! We're hit! Let's jump," said a rebel warrior. Out they jumped and into some water went Micco and the rest of the crew.

"We're never going to make it to Enniad," said a warrior. "Don't say that' said Micco as he came up gasping air. "We'll figure something out," he said. Micco and the other two rebels that he was with got to shore and began to walk through a jungle. "Let's find the craft," said Micco. "We can try and contact Kronogar from there," he said.

CHAPTER 3

"I love how this fire smells mother." Said Velaticcus as he sat on the floor by a fireplace. "Me too, son," said Alentina. "Will I ever be a great warrior like my father?" He asked. "You'll be even greater son." She said, as she now bent down and smiled, looking into Velaticcus's eyes. Unexpectedly, there was a knock at the door. "Who is it?" Asked Alentina. The door then burst open and what looked like a warrior with a green mask grabbed Alentina by the hair dragging her out. "Mother! Nooo!" cried Velaticcus. "Nooo!" he whimpered as he was suddenly awoken by hot soup that had been poured on his face. "Ah!" he yelled.

"You cry like a child!" said a voice. Velaticcus had been taken into a deep cave and was now locked inside a cell.

"You need to eat," said the voice again. "I'm going to have your head once I get out!" Threatened Velaticcus. "Not with your legs broken," said the creature which he could now see was a female wearing a veil. "If you ever plan on walking again, you'll need to eat first," she said. "And who are you?' he asked. "That's none of your concern said the unknown female" "Eat Velaticcus," she said. "No," said Velaticcus. Velaticcus then spit on the female in front of him. "You dare!" she growled angrily as she wiped her face in disgust. The female then unlocked the door, which was between them and let out a large whistle.

Immediately a mob of Xusapians (Xusapians were an indigenous tribe of Zenkovians that existed in the last jungle of Zenkov which was about the size of our Alaska) came in and lifted Velaticcus carrying him out of the cave and began to tie his wrists. "Give him the water treatment!" she commanded." "With pleasure!" said a member of the mob, then they took Velaticcus to a nearby stream and began to dunk his head in and out of the stream and laughed each time he gasped. "Say, you're sorry!" said the female. "No.," said Velaticcus. "I'm sorr" ...Velaticcus's head went underwater. "I can't hear you, what did you say?" said the female joyfully.

"I said!" Down went his head again. "I'm sorry!" cried Velaticcus. "And you're going to eat like a good boy, right?" asked the female. "Yes!

I'll eat too!" blubbered the red-faced Velaticcus. "Good!" said the female.

CONTACT

Beep!

A device on Kronogar's belt went off.

The group were now traveling back to the hallow tree and decided they would camp on the other side for the night since they were all so tired now. "Your father must have explored different times on Earth," said Meagles.

When Edwin had found the object that the tracking device had led him to, it was a weapon that Heronis had built and hid on Earth in the past. While Heronis had been exploring Earth, he had also seen different futures and planned out when and where his daughter and Meagles would find the violin and the weapon.

"He must have known he was going to die then," mumbled Lady Inera. "I don't think you can change when you die," said Meagles. "When we go, we go," he said. "On Zenkov," said Kronogar as he was now talking through the device that was on his belt to Micco. "It'll have to wait." Said Kronogar. "Just hang tight" he said were going to call it a night and continue tomorrow.

We found the device." He said.

Then Kronogar beeped his device off.

The group then went back through the hallow tree, and Edwin was no longer invisible.

"So, how did I die?" Asked Gordan now looking at his grandson. "In your sleep," said Edwin. "Well, that's good," said Gordon. "You don't get to see that every day." Said Meagles, as he looked up into the darkened sky. The Aurora Borealis looking lights were becoming visible now, and everyone was now slowly going to sleep as they continued chatting around a fire.

LOOKING

"Keep going straight," said Armant. He had been searching for Lady Inera all this time since he left planet Zenkov. Some warriors under his command who were also looking for Velaticcus reported him dead. They had come to the place where he had been thrown out of the pod by Kronogar and only found his teeth and bloodstains, which led them to believe he had been eaten by some wild animals. They were not aware of the isolated tribe that existed in the last jungle of Zenkov.

"Lady Inera will be my wife when we find her," said Armant. If Kronogar is alive, he will be executed for treason, and that means I am in charge." he said.

HISTORY

When Velaticcus took his father's place in ruling planet Zenkov, he was gifted a beautiful wife from an unknown place. His servants had found her wandering in the kingdom, speaking in a strange dialect. She was captured, dressed in new clothing after beauty treatments and forced to marry Velaticcus. Royal Zenkovians had a culture where their first-born child needed to be a boy; if the firstborn was not a boy, the ruler was shamed. The wife that Velaticcus was given had a baby girl, after being shamed he decided to kill her. Velaticcus's servants had given away the child and taken the mother to an unknown place and flung her off a cliff. "Tasty?" asked the veiled female. "Yes," said Velaticcus quickly, not wanting to suffer through another water treatment." "Good," said the female. "It's time for you to see my face," said the female. The female then lifted her veil and looked at Velaticcus. "Familiar?" she asked. "I know those eyes," he said as he stared into her face.

"No, you don't," she said.

DIFFERENT TUNES

"It must be played at a certain tune," said Meagles. The group was up and walking again, taking the weapon back to the lab. "How much longer?" asked Edwin. "I'm starved." He said. "Almost there," said Lady Inera. Then suddenly, a light appeared over her, and like lightning, she was zapped and gone!

"Oh no! cried Meagles. "They've taken her!" He cried. Lady Inera had been teleported onto a Zenkovian pod and whisked *away*. "Hide!" yelled Kronogar. The remaining group hid behind some trees and waited until they felt safe. They didn't want to risk losing

43

the weapon. "He won't harm her, "said Kronogar. He wants a healthy son too much to hurt her, he said. "How did they find us?' Asked Meagles. "Velaticcus must have put a tracking device on her somehow, probably when her father had made the truce with him," said Kronogar.

STAIRWAY

"Time to go," said Micco. "The secret base is with the Xusapians," he said. "The Xusapians?" asked one of the warriors. "Yes," said Micco. "They are the last free Zenkovians that live in the last jungle on Zenkov," said Micco. "Wow," said the Warrior. "I thought all the resources were gone," he said. "They are gone, well, most of them." Replied Micco, "What's the jungle like?" Asked the other warrior. "Oh, you'll see." Said Micco. "And you're going to like the food too," he said. The three walked on and on through the polluted wastelands of Zenkov carrying large walking sticks and the little food that was left from the wreckage. Finally, they came to a large spiral stairway in the middle of nowhere. The stairway led to nothing and at the top was what looked like a small black trumpet. Micco climbed up the stairs and blew the trumpet three times, waited about five seconds, and blew it three more times. "I'm sure that's right," he said aloud then he invited the other two warriors to sit with him at the top.

45

"They'll be here soon." Said Micco. Finally, after what felt like hours, a green, egg-shaped pod with beaming lights arrived at the stairs, and the three went inside greeted by an unknown Zenkovian wearing a hooded cloak.

"Welcome," said the Zenkovian. "These are my two young apprentices," said Micco, proudly introducing the warriors to the hooded Zenkovian. "Excellent." said the hooded Zenkovian as he bowed. "You're going to like the motherland," he said to the warriors. "You'll finally get to see where Zenkovians really come from. "And guess what Micco," said the cloaked Zenkovian with a gleam. "We have him! His very Immanti found him!" "Really?" asked Micco. "Karma has a way of doing things," he said.

"Yes, it does." agreed the cloaked Zenkovian.

FORGOTTEN MEMORIES

"Here drink this," said the female as she handed a rusty grey cup to Velaticcus. "It should help you remember," she said. "Remember what?" asked Velaticcus. "Drink, and you'll find out," said the woman. "Is it poison?" he asked. "Just drink it!" said the woman. "Fine!" said Velaticcus. Velaticcus drank the warm beverage and fainted. The potion put him into a deep sleep like a coma, and he began to dream of the memories he had lost. He dreamt about the day his father had executed his mother. He was eight years old the day his father sent out his warriors to hunt his mother down. His mother, Alentina, had tried to escape from her husband and had taken Velaticcus with her. They had gone into one of the last villages in Zenkov that Cykunth (Velaticcus's tyrant father) had not yet enslaved and tried to raise Velaticcus there. Alentina did not want her son to become like her husband. When Cykunth finally found her, he ordered his warriors (who unknown to Cykunth were traitors) to throw her off a cliff. Cykunth then sent his son to a warrior school and began to form him into the cold-hearted tyrant that he became.

FUTURE PLANS

"I'll never love you!" yelled Lady Inera, "You're disgusting!" she said. "Oh, this isn't about love, dear, it's about royal blood and the royal baby that you're going to give me!" snickered Armant. "You're not a royal," said Lady Inera as two warriors were holding her wrists, forcing her to sit on a chair with handcuffs. "Oh yes I am, said Armant. Now that Velaticcus is dead and Kronogar is a traitor that makes me the ruler of Zenkov since poor Velaticcus didn't have a son. It's a shame he didn't accept that daughter of his and just create a new law that allowed females to rule, but that won't happen with you and I." said Armant, as he stared holes through Lady Inera while licking his lips. "Once we get married, I'll make the rules, and if we have a daughter, I won't be shamed like the fool before me," he said. "I'd rather die!" said Lady Inera. "Oh, don't be so dramatic," said Armant. "I've been told I'm rather easy on the eyes," he said now bringing his face to Lady Inera's face. "Someone obviously lied" huffed Lady Inera as she turned her face away from Armant. "With time, you'll learn to appreciate me, my dear," said Armant. "Now, for the wedding plans, make her pretty!" he said, looking at the warriors. "Yes, master." said the Warriors.

BACK AT THE LAB

Edwin, Meagles, Gordan, and Kronogar finally arrived back at the lab. "I'll head on back to Ahirine and get the part for the weapon, hopefully the Zenkovians haven't taken it," said Kronogar "Would you like to join me, Gordon, I could use some help." He said, "Sure," said Gordon. "We also need to rescue Lady Inera." The two took the pod and began to head back to planet Ahirine while Meagles and Edwin stayed on Enniad trying to figure out how to use the weapon Heronis had created.

THE JUNGLE

"We have arrived," said the cloaked Zenkovian. "Thank you," said Micco as he and his apprentices stepped off the ship. "Farewell," said the cloaked Zenkovian who bowed then shut the door to the pod and disappeared into the sky. They had been dropped off on top of a high building in the center of a huge city hidden by vast jungle. Below there was a bazaar and exotic Zenkovians walking in and out of different buildings with baskets filled with food and other items. The three could smell the delicious aroma of food that was baking in giant outdoor ovens. "Let's eat," said Micco as he started down a stairway leading into the building. When the three finally made it to the bottom of the building and outside, they bought some food and began to eat. "When we are done, we will change our clothes and then go and meet with Immanti," said Micco.

"Who's Immanti?" asked one of the warriors. "Immanti is our future," said Micco. "She is the one who is going to be different and put an end to all the slavery," he said. "That was delicious," said the old warrior finishing his bowl of soup and letting out a loud, satisfying burp. "My mother used to make me this," said Micco. "It's zini soup, made from pure, unpolluted jungle mice and green potatoes." He said. The three finished their tasty meals and bought some long cloaks from a nearby shop and changed, blending in with the rest of the indigenous Zenkovians. They walked a few miles and then entered a tunnel inside a mountain which then led them to a bench where they all sat and waited.

THE FUNERAL

He cried and cried. Tears of joy that is. Armant thought it would be best to hold a funeral for Kronogar and Velaticcus before his wedding to Lady Inera. "You're so fake," said Lady Inera, who was struggling to speak through a taped mouth. "I hate you," she scorned. She had been tied to a chair and forced to attend the event. "Thank you, friends!" Armant began to speak to the crowd that had gone to the funeral. "It brings me great pleasure to know that you are all under *my rule* now." he continued speaking. "Good riddance to Kronogar the traitor and Velaticcus the fool!" he said. "We are now better off, and may they rest in peace.

Let us go now and prepare for my wedding to my future ungrateful dashing bride!" he said as he blew Lady Inera a kiss. "All hail Armant!" said the crowd, "All hail Armant!"

XUSAPIA

Xusapia was the city in the last jungle of planet Zenkov. The city had been kept a secret since Velaticcus's grandfather had ruled over planet Zenkov. When Ceog (Velaticcus's great grandfather) was the ruler, he was the one who decided to evacuate planet Zenkov and go and look for other planets and enslave them.

Ceog thought Zenkov had become too polluted. Ceog had been a lazy ruler; he depended on his warriors to inform him of everything and so when he had asked them if there were any Zenkovians left on planet Zenkov, they told him "no" even though there were. Not too many warriors knew of Xusapia either since most were living on the mother ship or on the colonies that were on the planets they had enslaved. Since the rule of Ceog, planet Zenkov had been abandoned and used as a galactic dump.

Xusapia used most of the junk that had been dumped on it to its advantage and recycled the junk and continued to thrive in technology beneath the tyrant rulers and go undetected for generations. The Jungle was left untouched and forgotten.

AMAZING

"Here, wear this," said Kronogar as he tossed a hooded cloak to Gordon. The two had arrived to planet Ahirine and were now inside Heronis's old home looking for the other part of the weapon. "Ah, here it is!" said Kronogar. "How does it work?" asked Gordon. "This plugs into the inside of the violin, and it keeps it from taking you through time and then when the violin gets played with

this plugged into it, it somehow triggers the weapon, and it becomes a hundred times more explosive. "Amazing," said Gordan.
"Yea," said Kronogar. "How about you take this and head back to
Enniad, I'll take another pod from here and find Lady Inera." He
said, "Sounds like a plan," replied Gordon.

53

CHAPTER 4

"Welcome," said Immanti. Micco and his apprentices finally arrived at the village of the indigenous Xusapians.

"Thank you said Micco. "How are you doing?" he asked. Immanti was the daughter of Velaticcus that had been given away at birth. Velaticcus's servant had given her to a couple who were unable to bear children in the indigenous village far from the city of Xusapia. "I know how hard this must be for you," said Micco. Immanti knew that Velaticcus was her biological father.

"Oh, it's fine Micco, I can't miss something that I never had and besides Leo is my father.' She said. "Are we almost ready for the rebellion?' asked Micco. "Yes, the other rebels are going to gather, and then we will plan the attack." Said Immanti." Excellent! Said Micco with a warm smile. The indigenous Zenkovians and all the rebels who wanted to overthrow Velaticcus had been preparing for a rebellion. Having captured Velaticcus was not enough, though, even if they killed Velaticcus, Armant had become the new tyrant. They needed to go to war since there were still many Zenkovians who liked living under a dictatorship.

BORED

"When do you think they'll be back? Asked Edwin "Oh, I don't know," said Meagles. Since Gordon and Kronogar had gone to retrieve the other part to the weapon and rescue Lady Inera, Meagles and Edwin had been figuring out how the violin worked. They discovered that it could be played like a regular violin without it taking someone back in time or to the future. It was only that specific tune that Gordon had taught Edwin would send him through space travel. "When they arrive, we'll let them know of our plan," said Meagles. They had been discussing how Gordon and Edwin would be sent back after they used the weapon in the rebellion. "Once the weapon is used, your grandfather will go back the way he came, and so will you. It's amazing how Heronis knew of these things and how perfectly they fit like a puzzle." Said Edwin. "Yes, he was a great and intelligent leader said Meagles.

WEDDING CRASHERS

"Come on, my dear," said Armant. "The time has come, let's not make a scene." He said. Lady Inera had been forced into a wedding dress and had some stylish heels super glued to her feet. She had been fighting and kicking the shoes off while trying to resist marrying Armant. She had now been calmed by being forced to take some medication which subdued her, and she was now being forced to walk down the aisle since Armant had threatened to kill some innocent children if she refused. "You're a beast," she said.

"Oh yes I am, wait till tonight," he said. "You'll get to see the real beast!" he said.

All at once, Gordon appeared. "Hey!" he yelled then suddenly when Armant was distracted, Kronogar bashed in a window right behind Lady Inera and carried her out as Gordan ran back out to meet him and they all jumped into a pod and beamed away.

"Get her! Yelled Armant as he and his guests all ran out of the chapel and rushed into other pods. "What took you guys so long!" said Lady Inera. "We had to get the other part to the violin," said Kronogar. "I'll lose them in the Jungle," said Kronogar. Kronogar then alerted Micco on a communication device letting him know he was with Lady Inera heading in their direction.

REVELATIONS

"I am your daughter," said Immanti as she looked at Velaticcus. "Do you remember now" she asked. "I remember," said Velaticcus. "I had forgotten what my father had done." He said. "And you have become much like him," said Immanti. "Immanti!" shouted Micco. "Immanti!" he said as he ran into the room where she was talking with Velaticcus. "Kronogar is coming this way! We need to set off the alarms!" "Others are following him." Some loud horns were then blown throughout the area warning of the possible attack, and the indigenous Zenkovians began to hide while others prepared to fight. "He is working on losing them, but we need to prepare in case he doesn't," said Micco.

SHOOT STRAIGHT

"Can't you shoot straight?" grumbled Armant as he stammered behind the gunner in the pod that was chasing his escaped bride. "I am doing my best!" cried the gunner. 'Open the door! Said Armant to another Zenkovian. The door was opened, and Armant grabbed the gunner by the collar and flung him out! "Ahhh!" cried the gunner. Armant then sat in the gunner's seat and attempted to shoot the pod his bride was escaping in. Suddenly, another pod appeared and was chasing after Armant and began to shoot at him. Boom! A hole was shot in the engine, and Armant's pod went crashing down and exploded into pieces. "They got him!" said Gordon. "Great!" said Lady Inera. It was Micco.

After the alarms had gone off around the Indigenous Zenkovians, Micco had taken a fighter pod that had been kept hidden in the village, caught up with Armant and taken him down. The two pods went back to the village and landed, then a crowd gathered and cheered. Micco had been communicating with Immanti all this time. "He is here," said Micco as he now led Kronogar into the cave where Velaticcus was being kept. "I'm amazed he survived," said Kronogar. "His own daughter found him," said Micco. "Well, isn't that something said Kronogar. "Well, he is her father, after all," said Kronogar. "I think she should decide what's best," he said.

GOOD ENDINGS

Time passed, and Velaticcus was soon able to walk again, with a cane. His daughter, Immanti, felt pity on her father since she believed he had become so terrible because of her grandfather and decided to let him live. Velaticcus did feel guilty soon after regaining his memory and asked his daughter to forgive him. The indigenous Zenkovians came out of hiding and joined the other Zenkovians in the other colonies across the different planets that had been conquered through Velaticcus's tyrannical rule, and the slaves were freed. Many of the slaves returned to their old homes or stayed. The Zenkovians also decided that Immanti was the proper ruler and she decided to start cleaning planet Zenkov from generations of trash that had been piled up on the planet. Finally, after months of being away from Earth, Gordan and Edwin went back to the lab and decided it was time for them to go home.

STAYING BEHIND

"I will miss you all," said Meagles. Lady Inera, Kronogar, Gordan and Edwin were all back in the Vonkernera like world that was created by Heronis's Vonkern scientists. They were taking one last look at the beautiful lights in the sky. They had decided that once Gordan and Edwin returned to Earth, Edwin would go back with the violin and Meagles (who brought along a few of the other Vonkern survivors) would stay in the Vonkernera like planet hidden on Earth and start over. "Here, take this." Said Lady Inera who gave some hallow tree seeds to Gordon." They'll be safer with you said Lady Inera. After Edwin, Meagles, and Gordon said their goodbyes and returned to Earth, Lady Inera and Kronogar decided they would use the weapon to blow up the lab so that Earth would remain undiscovered. They still had been the only ones to have known about Earth since Lady Inera's father had discovered it with his scientists. All the hallow trees that had grown on Enniad were destroyed, and the only ones remaining were the seeds that were given to Gordan. When Gordon returned to where he had come, some fellow soldiers soon found him; coincidentally one was named Heronis. The group of soldiers decided to camp by the hallow tree for the night and chop the tree down, not knowing it was a magical tree and burned the wood. Gordon took part of the remaining wood that had not been burnt, and later he carved a violin out of it which he would later give to his son.

LIGHTS

When Edwin returned to Earth, he awoke back in the cottage that his grandfather and father had built for him when he was eight. He sat up and noticed the fire was still burning in front of him. It was as though he had never left. Edwin glanced at the violin that his grandfather had given him and thought about playing a tune on it, but then he reached in his back pocket and took out a photo of his grandfather and smiled. Edwin then sat back and shut his eyes, fell asleep and dreamt of some wonderful lights that looked like the Aurora Borealis.

The Petrified Kingdom of the Gourges

Book 2

CHAPTER 1

"She's escaped! The Princess is gone!" cried the servant, "I have no clue as to how!" he whimpered as he bowed fearfully before the Great King Giorgio. "Find her!" bellowed the Great King "I don't care what you have to do but find my daughter!" It was wartime. The Ruler of the Kingdom of the Endless Mountains had arranged for his eldest daughter, Nieve, to marry the Prince of the Mythical Valley. The union would unite the armies to help fight the cursed gourges of the Petrified Kingdom.

"Gurgle. Gurgle" breathed the gourge. "GURGLE, GRRR!" it said again in its sick voice. The Princess blinked, and then she noticed the twinkling of the stars. Suddenly, she realized she was not in her room and then there it was, that awkward stench again of something ancient and dry but not the typical dry that one would normally think. It was the type of dryness that happens to a soul that has experienced so much that the life drained out of it. "I thought you were a nightmare said the Princess. "I was once a dream," stated the gourge. "But no, I am surely real. Very, very real," laughed the gourge. "Well, what do you want?" asked the Princess. "What do I want?" snickered the gourge sarcastically. "Surely you recall that it was you that came seeking me," said the gourge, through his seaweed green eyes. The gourge then sat up and slid a rusty, brown key at the feet of the Princess.

"That looks familiar," thought the Princess as she slowly lifted herself up from the cold hard ground. "I think I remember now," said the Princess.

What the Princess forgot was that a few nights ago she and her sisters (Samara and Anne) had been playing in the castle in the forbidden rooms that their father had told them over and over a million times not to enter. Nieve and Anne were trying to hide from Samara when suddenly the two went under a bed to hide.

Anne bumped her head on something wooden. "Ouch!" yelled Anne. "Something like a rock just hit my head!" she cried. "Really!" said Nieve. "Well if your head wasn't so big you wouldn't have that problem," she muttered.

"There you are!" Shouted Samara, the youngest of the three, "My babies!" she chuckled with joy. "Oh my God!" said Nieve. "Well if you hadn't made so much noise, she wouldn't have found us," said Anne. "Look what I found," said the youngest. Samara smiled as she waved a rusty brown key in her tiny little hand. "Where did you get that!?" gasped Nieve. "Over here!" said Samara. Then she ran out of the room, down the stairs, down the hallway and into the inner courtyard into the garden. It was a door. "That's where you got this key," asked Anne. "Yes," said Samara. "It was in that little hole," she said, pointing innocently at a keyhole. The door

was concealed by some large exotic looking plants which had existed before they were born. The girls were living in an ancient castle
which was built by their great grandfather's great grandfather. (It
probably existed when dinosaurs roamed the earth) Anyway, Nieve
pried the key from Samara's tiny defeated hand and unlocked the
door. It was like a basement; it had a cold, dark, steep stairway.
The girls took a lantern from another forbidden room that their father told them not to go into and lit it with a candle. They walked
slowly and quietly down the narrow stairs being careful, avoiding
capture by one of the servants. There must have been at least a
hundred steps because from the time it took them to enter to the
time, they finally reached the bottom, it had been a least twenty
minutes. "A bush," said Anne. "We came all this way for a bush?"
she panted.

The girls discovered a small tree. Unlike all other trees, this one
was a portal, and unlike other trees, this tree grew in darkness, and
it glowed. If this tree became exposed to light, it would have died.

"Wow it sure smells tasty," said Samara.

"I'm so hungry," she moaned as she suddenly tore off a piece of
fruit from one of the branches and ate it. "No!" yelled Nieve, but it
was too late. Samara was in another place. The fruit She had eat-
en had sent her through a magic portal.

In fact, she had unknowingly entered The Petrified Kingdom of the Gourges.

THE OLD STORY

There was an old story told in the girls' family which passed on from generation to generation. The story was about a beautiful Kingdom that used to exist with incredibly beautiful people. Rumor had it that the people were so beautiful that they looked like angels. Then something terrible happened which turned that Kingdom into stone. A plague or a curse from an evil witch turned the beautiful people into hideous creatures, like zombies. It was also rumored that in the beginning of the family line, one of those creatures was part of the royal family.

GRANDMOTHER

"Grandma!" shrieked Sherrie. "Grandma what happened?

Was it the neighbor's beastly dog?" Sherrie's grandmother had a sucking shoulder wound that was bleeding black fluid in place of blood. "Ohhh!" I was bitten by a strange nosferatu of some sort," said the grandma.

"Nosferatu?" asked Sherrie.

"But nosferatu's are not real grandma," said Sherrie. Sherrie's grandmother had been in the woods gathering herbs and berries for dinner that evening for a pie. As the sun was just beginning to set, something approached her which did appear to be a strange nosferatu or a slow vampire.

Since it was dim out, Sherrie's grandmother (I shall call her Abbey) could not make out who or what was approaching her (also because of old age her vision was fading), all Abbey heard was what sounded like a sick person approaching her. "Are you alright?" asked Abbey, "Do you need help?" said the kind old lady. "Rarrrr! "said the dingbat vampire. The foggy-brained vampire bit Abbey on the shoulder instead of the neck, "Rarrrr!!" mumbled the strange nosferatu as it munched on Abbey's bitten off shoulder.

To the slow vampire, the piece of shoulder was a delicious delicacy, just think of the savory flavor of your favorite beef dish with mushrooms and garlic. That is what was going through this nosferatu's mind. It did not see a poor helpless older lady trying to get away; it saw an upright sizzling steak trying to getaway. "No! No!" cried Sherrie. "Oh, grandmother, oh, grandmother!" Sherrie ran inside, grabbed a cloth, and began to put pressure on her grandmother's wound with the cloth. The two ladies went inside the house and locked the door. The horrible nosferatu wandered back into the woods in pursuit of a deer that it noticed after it bit Abbey.

PETRIFY THIS

"La! Laaa! La! La! La! La!" sang Samara. "La!

La! Laaaaaaa!" sang the girl. The child had been walking through the cobblestone streets of the old town of the Petrified Kingdom for hours now. The town was grey, quiet, and vacant. There was no sun out, just grey. You could hear a pin dropping where there used to be sounds of laughter and music coming from the citizens of the Petrified Kingdom where people used to gather to dance and trade and socialize. "Is anyone here?" whimpered Samara, "Hello?" The girl was getting tired and hungry. Samara climbed up on a wooden bench that was up against an old dress shop and curled up in a ball. "I'm so tired," she moaned. Samara closed her eyes and fell asleep. Unexpectedly, a cold breeze began to blow. "There she is," said a gourge. "Oh, good," said a different gourge. "Let us hurry for it is almost time!" said one of the gourges. Two gourges had been trying to find Samara since she had entered the Kingdom. Give me the herbs, hurry!" said the first gourge. The second gourge handed the first gourge a bag of purple herbs and placed it over the child's nose so that she could breathe them in. The herbs that the gourges had given Samara to inhale were sleeping herbs. This specific type of herb would keep people from waking up and suppress their hunger for a few hours and prevent them from having nightmares. "Let us leave now," said the second gourge. The first gourge, which was the bigger one, lifted Samara up and placed her over its shoulder and began to run. "Hurry!

Get out of here!" said the second gourge.

"I'll stay here just in case," he said as he drew a sword...

BACK IN THE CASTLE

"You bite it first," said Anne. "No, you," said Nieve. The sisters had been fighting over who would bite the fruit from the tree ever since poor Samara had disappeared. "Let's both do it at the same time," said Nieve.

"Alright on three," said Anne "One...two...three!" "Puff!" The girls had disappeared from the castle. "Huh?" said Nieve. "Where are we?" Stated Anne in amazement. "Good question you twerp," "said Nieve annoyed. The girls were now in the Petrified Kingdom.

The girls got up and began to walk.

For hours they walked, and as the girls walked, they noticed the elegant buildings that surrounded them along with the colors and the faded aroma of flowers that used to exist. They had gone in and out some of the old abandoned shops and played dress-up as they explored. "It must have been beautiful here ...said Anne remorsefully. "Yes... it must have..." agreed her sister.

"Oh, look... she was here," said Nieve. There was a pink torn piece of cloth on a wooden bench which belonged to Samara's dress.

"Samara!" Samara!" The sisters began to call and look around "Shush! Quiet!" bellowed a gourge, which suddenly came from out of an alley. It was the second gourge that had stayed behind when the other gourge took Samara away.

"Come with me," he said.

"Who are you?" asked Nieve.

"No time to explain, please come with me!" said the gourge. "I don't feel safe ...have you seen our sister?" asked Nieve. "Yes, I have seen her; she is safe with my brother," replied the gourge hastily. "You must follow me now the witch may be coming soon!" said the desperate gourge.

The girls finally gave in and began to follow the creature out of the old town of the Petrified Kingdom into a swamp.

THE SWAMP

The swamp that the creature and the girls were traveling through was to the east of the old town which was in the center of The Petrified Kingdom. To the southwest of The Petrified Kingdom beyond the Frozen Mountains, where other evil creatures existed, was the witch's portal. It was a portal created by her to travel to the human world so that she could hide from the gourges after she had cursed them. The witch was a jealous old hag who had envied the citizens of the Petrified Kingdom. She used to stare at them from afar envious of their beauty and wanted them dead. Before the witch hated them, she had a brother who was her only family, but he was an evil warlock who would bring fear to the people. Her brother, Alexander, would kidnap children and drain their life so that he could grow more powerful.

The warlock wanted to rule over the Kingdom.

Tired of the warlock, the people of the Petrified Kingdom gathered an army and hunted him down. The warlock's sister was unknown to the people; she had been born hideous and so would not go out in public. Her brother was her only gateway to the outside world, and so when the people captured and burned her brother, the witch grew hateful and placed a curse on all the people for revenge. Many of the citizens died from the curse.

The curse was like a disease, and if you survived passed a certain point, you became a gourge which to the gourges advantage, you also became stronger but frightening like a werewolf. Then there were those who did not fully transform into gourges or die. The survivors who did not fully become gourges or die became like zombies, rotting, and wanting to eat flesh and dumb. Unknown to the witch, there was one family of survivors that the curse could not affect.

It was a family of white witches.

When the evil witch placed her curse on the Kingdom, this family created a portal through a small tree to escape to the human world, and they also made it so that if they ever wanted to return, they had to eat the fruit of the tree. The only way to lift the curse was to mix the blood of the witch with the blood of a white witch and drink it. "Are you going to harm us?" muttered Anne as she waddled like a duck in mud. "No," said the gourge. I am trying to save you. "From the witch?" asked Nieve, "Yes, from the witch," said the gourge. "Can you please explain what is going on" pleaded Anne. "The witch wants to capture you and your sisters" The gourge began to explain. "Why?" asked Nieve. "Because she doesn't want the curse of the Petrified Kingdom to be lifted... you see, we need just a drop of your blood mixed with the witch's blood to lift the curse" Explained the gourge. "Why our blood?" asked Nieve. "Your family isn't affected by the witch's curse," said the gourge.

Along they went through the murky shadowy swamp for what seemed like days until finally one of the sister's collapsed. "We shall stop here for the night." Stated the gourge as he looked at the girls who were exhausted and drenched in sweat and insects. "Finally," ...one of them mumbled. The gourge started a fire with some plants then he and the girls went to sleep.

OFF WITH HIS HEAD

"Bring me the Knight!!" Commanded the King in his angered voice. "But your GREATNESS...it was necessary..." said Sir Harrist the Knight in command after the King's most trusted Knight, Sir Vallah. "I don't care!" said the King. "I gave an order, and my orders are not to be questioned! They are to be followed" muttered King Giorgio. (At least that is who appeared to be King Giorgio) The Knight bowed and removed himself from the presence of the King. Dumbfounded by the King's recent odd behavior, he went out to organize a party to find the Knight that had fled.

The King then walked off to his bedroom and locked the door, careful that no one was watching. He then got on his knees by the floor near his bed and knocked on the floor. "Ah, here it is" The King whispered to himself. King Giorgio quietly lifted a piece of loose wood from the floor, which was about a foot in length and reached down with his hairy arm (which was like sheep fur) into a hidden compartment.

He lifted out a fruit, which was the exact same fruit found on the tree to the Petrified Kingdom and bit it. Poof! The King was gone!

See, what happened was that the witch had kidnapped the King and taken him to the human world. Days earlier before the girls discovered the plant portal to the Petrified Kingdom, the witch had disguised herself as an old lady seeking employment in the Kingdom.

News had spread throughout the Kingdom that the King was going to throw a great banquet for the wedding of the Princess, and he ordered his Knights to gather the finest cooks throughout the land with a sample of their best dishes. The witch, pretending to be a cook cast a spell on some horse feces and offered it as her best dish to the King. The King, because of the magic of the spell, tasted it and thought "Mm... this is the best I have ever had" The poor King, fooled by witchcraft thought he was eating chocolate and seriously thought it tasted great" The King hired the witch and made her head of his kitchen.

After poor King Giorgio had welcomed the witch to his castle the witch cooked up another evil spell, this time in liquid form (better not to mention where that came from) and served it to everyone in the castle making them sick with dysentery and putting them to sleep which then gave her just enough time to put a curse on the

King (the same curse from the Petrified Kingdom) and transfer him through her portal that she had created to flee the citizens of the Petrified Kingdom after she had cursed them.

THE KNIGHT THAT FLED

Away he rode, swift into the night with his big red beard, the King's most trusted knight. Sir Vallah, stole the King's fastest horse and fled out of the Kingdom of the Endless Mountains. He had snuck away while his fellow knights had nodded off to bed after drinking the mint ale that came from the knights' garden.

The King's most valued knights lived a privileged life. They had their own place set aside from all the other knights in the Kingdom. Their estates were much like our modern-day barracks but with a more mid-evil touch to it and each Knight having a wing to himself.

The knights had a bit of land that came with their estate where they could have a barn for their horses and plant a garden if they liked. Once a Knight was granted to live there, he could choose to skip a battle if it was not too severe. For a knight to achieve this privileged life, they had to kill at least a hundred men per battle continuously for at least ten battles. The Knights of the Kingdom of the Endless mountains were the most feared, respected, highly skilled and alcohol tolerant men in all the land. The knights training began at the age of nine.

Once a young boy could read and write, they began in a selective mandatory draft which was carried out every two to five years, depending on if the Kingdom was short on knights. The other knights did not have any housing like the privileged ones and had a salary that they received depending on how valuable they were, (the more slays and skills that a knight had the better), and they also worked part-time in a labor job like a blacksmith or piemaker. The privileged knights who lived in the Knights Estates did not have to work at a part-time job; instead, their salary came from how well they trained the knights below them. Each one of the privileged knights had fifty to one-hundred knights below him. Once a knight was at least fifty, he became a sort of schoolteacher to the youngest of the knights just entering knighthood and trained them on the basics of knighthood until he felt he could move on to the next level of training.

THE WITCH'S PORTAL

Now, to clear up the confusion if things do not make sense to you yet. The portal that the witch had created also led her to the human world (In case you do not remember, I almost forgot). In fact, that portal she created led her right to the United States while the family of the white witches created their portal; it gave them a short cut to the Kingdom of the Endless Mountains. The witch created a humble cottage for herself in some woods and lived an entire lifetime when she had vanished. The witch lived a normal human lifestyle. She fell in love, met a man (who was an inmate actually).

When the man was released, he married the witch not knowing she was a witch and they had children, grew old, and then she poisoned him when she no longer found him attractive and went on to have grandchildren.

Abbey was the name she had given herself. And she now had the cursed King (who unfortunately did not fully transform into a gourge) wandering around helplessly in her back yard.

The King, barely able to remember that he needed the witch's blood mixed with the blood of a white witch to change back, tried to kill the witch one evening when he spotted her looking like a piece of steak gathering berries (Even though the witch looked like an upright steak to the King, in his slowed pitiful mind he could still recognize her rotten voice). The King almost got her, but then he noticed (like a person easily distracted by shiny things) a deer and followed the deer back into the woods (ooh, pretty, thought the King).

After the witch had taken the King through the portal, (before he thought she was a sizzling steak), she took a piece of the King's hair and used it in a spell to transform herself to look like him. The witch gave out new orders to the King's knights, ordering them to prepare for war against their allies, the gourges of the Petrified Kingdom, and the Kingdom of the Mythical Valley. King Giorgio had known about the tree that was at the bottom of his Kingdom and had only told his most trusted Knight (Sir Vallah) about it.

Amazingly and coincidentally, Samara had dreamt about the Kingdom. The girls were not aware that they were white witches. The girls occasionally experienced strange dreams which unknown to them were premonitions or warnings. Nights before Samara had found the key in the door which led her to the magic tree, Samara had dreamt about it. Samara had experienced déjà vu the entire day she found the key and led her sisters to the tree portal.

THE WORLD BENEATH

"Has she awoken yet?" asked Petry the Vonkern.

"No," said Joseph, (Joseph was the gourge that had carried Samara away on his shoulder) "Any sign of James?" asked Joseph. "No, not yet," said Petry. (James was the gourge who found the Princesses in the Petrified Kingdom and led them into the swamp)

The Vonkern was a creature as big as a gourge but looked like a frog and turquoise and silver in color, quite beautiful; in fact, and their skin was tough like the skin of an alligator. Unlike a frog, Vonkerns did not eat flies and were exceptionally talented cooks; their eyes were shaped like ovals, large and blue. Their eyes were the deepest bluest eyes you could imagine and could see three times the distance of any human. One of their best meals were baked mushrooms with a delicious buttery substance that also came from pine trees found only in their native land.

Prior to the curse on the Petrified Kingdom, the Vonkerns were regular visitors to the Old Town where every year at the beginning of fall, everyone from everywhere would gather to celebrate when the moon would turn light blue and cooking, and music competitions began. The mushrooms that the Vonkerns used, found only in their native home, (which was underground) were bigger than loaves of bread and gold in color.

The underground home of the Vonkerns was deep in the ground, and there was only one way you could get in; it was through a concealed hole at the roots of the hallow tree in a hidden cave that was thousands of years old. The home of the Vonkerns was like another planet.

Vonkern Land was otherworldly like our Alaska. It only had lights above that resembled distance stars but could not be stars because it was underground. See, it was a giant cave, but the Land of the Vonkerns did not look like a cave. There was a large sandy beach with white sand which glowed, it was always nighttime, but somehow you were able to see clearly. It seemed to be like an eternal afternoon with the temperature always warm.

It was a wonderful place to comfort hurting joints.

There was also a vast desert which was as big as Texas, and like a desert, it was hot, and strangely there were even camels there. The camels were black and furrier than our camels and a bit larger too. Then, there was the long stretching scent of the pines which smelled for miles. Most of the Vonkerns lived in the pine forest close to the beach where the entrance to their land was. Vonkerns loved to burn firewood and so as soon as you smelled burning pine you knew you had entered the Land of the Vonkerns. Fireflies were also abundant in their land, and so was the sound of chirping night birds and crickets. Samara had been sleeping soundly by a warm fireplace in the home of Petry the Vonkern.

The young Princess was dreaming away, forbidden to have nightmares because of the herbs she had inhaled earlier.

Meanwhile, Petry was preparing his best-baked mushrooms for when she awoke.

BUNNY STEW AND NIGHTMARES

"You're it! "Exclaimed Nieve. Nieve turned around and ran through a large hall and up some stairs.

She noticed something strange, everything darkened around her, and some torches that were on the sides of the stone walls suddenly lit as though by magic. The fire from the torches was a flaming blue, and she could smell the scent of rich firewood coming from a different room. "I'm going to find you!" Said Anne from a distance.

Nieve followed the smell of firewood into a bedroom she never knew existed in her father's castle. "Well, this is strange," thought Nieve. Before her was a fire burning in an empty room which she had never seen. Nieve went in and then suddenly an old lady in a long black cloak with white eyes who looked about a hundred years old appeared. "Who are you?" asked Nieve in a near whisper. "Oh, come closer, dear and I shall tell you," Said the old lady, in an untrusting and dry voice. Nieve, as though caught in a trance, went closer to the old lady.

*"Closer dear," grinned the old lady. "Bahahahaahahahahaha!!!
"Chuckled the old hag as she grabbed Nieve by the arm and then*

pushed her into the fire. "Ahhh!" screamed Nieve as she suddenly awoke by icy water splashing on her face that Anne had poured on her.

"Wake up!" said Anne as she hovered over her.

It had all been a bad dream. "Oh my God," said Nieve as she rubbed her eyes. "It's time to eat," said Anne. Anne and the gourge James had gone hunting earlier while Nieve was left sleeping heavily by smoldering fire embers. They had captured some swamp bunnies with arrows they had carved from branches and cooked them in a stew with wild potatoes they had found growing nearby and mixed herbs. Swamp bunnies were just like the bunnies in our world except they were aquatic and lived on both land and water and they ate both plants and fish.

Swamp bunnies still had fur but more like the fur of a platypus and webbed feet and they still hopped around and had large ears.

"Mmm, mm, what is this?" asked Nieve as Anne handed her a bowl of swamp bunny stew.

"No time for questions," said James. "We need to leave this place as soon as you are done. We cannot leave any trace that we were here. We need to make it to the hallow tree in time, or we will be locked out for months," he said. Nieve ate the soup (It was so creamy and delicious.) Nieve enjoyed every bite of it, and it really hit the spot. She had not eaten since they entered the portal. The girls covered the remains of the fire, making sure the area looked untouched and then began to follow the gourge to the hallow tree that led to the World Beneath.

THE BARGE HOUND

It sniffed and sniffed, desperately trying to pick up the scent of the girls. It was a hound but not just any hound, a BARGE HOUND. The barge hound was a canine bear-like creature; it looked like a mix between a black bear and a wolf. It had the head of a wolf with a smaller snout, but the body resembled that of a bear and silver in color with blood-red eyes and a nose which could pick up scent for miles. The barge hound stood about seven feet when standing on all fours. It had been searching for the Princesses all this time.

CHAPTER 2

Poof! The deer chased by the King suddenly disappeared into a tree.

"Argg! Ughgh!

Grr! Gurgle gurgle," sulked the slow mind depraved King in starving frustration as he continued to chase the deer that had distracted him from killing the witch. "Poof" The King disappeared after the deer. The deer was not really a deer; it was a Knight (Sir Vallah who had fled earlier in the story) he had volunteered to go on a rescue mission after the King and bring him back to the Kingdom of the Endless Mountains. The Knight had noticed that the King was not himself and consulted advice from the wizard of the Mythical Valley. Together, they realized that the King was not the King but an imposter. The wizard, Venton cast a spell on Sir Vallah which transformed him into a deer.

As the two fell back through the portal back into the other world, the wizard had been waiting by the entire time. "Oh Finally!" exclaimed the wizard "*Alliiiee... Challiiieee... gala... moo... shaaa!*" chanted the wizard as he waved his green shiny wand around the deer, transforming it back into the Knight.

"Never again!" Sobbed Sir Vallah as he became human again. (He had not enjoyed being a deer) "Here!" said the wizard as he looked away in disgust and kicked the knight's clothes and armor back at him.

Meanwhile, the King had been knocked out cold since he ran his head straight into a branch as he came out of the portal. Out of nowhere, a large night bird landed on the wizard's hand.

"chirp, chirp, chirpity, chirp chirp," said the green and blue night bird. The bird who was the wizard's lifelong friend and pet had been flying around the Petrified Kingdom searching for the girls. "A barge hound, you say?" asked the wizard. "Well, that's not good!!" said the wizard.

BAKED MUSHROOMS

"Hmmm," thought Samara as she sleepily opened her eyes and looked around. The child thought she was dreaming. "Nieve?

Anne?

Daddy?" she asked as she hesitantly began to sit up.

"Hello sweetie," said Petry cautiously trying not to startle the child as he and Joseph entered the room.

"Who are you?" asked Samara. "I'm Petry," said Petry. And I am Joseph," said Joseph "Are you a frog?" asked Samara. "No, I'm a

Vonkern," said Petry. "You're a big pretty frog," said Samara ignoring what he said now looking up at Joseph and then at the plate of food he had in his hands. "What's that?" asked the hungry child. "It's supper for you," said Joseph" Come, let us go in here," said Joseph as he and Petry took the youngster's hand and led her into the kitchen. The three all sat down around the old round table and began to eat the delicious buttery mushrooms and drink minty tea with milk. They ate until they were all satisfied.

THE HALLOW TREE

Now, back to the hallow tree.

It was a strange tree, indeed, and no one knew how it came to be. As far as anyone knew, it had always existed.

The tree was hiding away in a valley inside a vast cool cave beyond the murky swamp; it was in some mountain cave where you had only one shot at getting in every six months. A large hole would appear right at the roots of the tree and would only stay open for three days. The tree had a white trunk with a circumference of about fifteen feet.

Its branches extended up to the cave ceiling to the point to where your eyes could not see the end of them. Many night birds nestled in the tree and a yellow fruit about the size of an apricot that looked more like berries grew from the branches which supplied food for the birds. Joseph had made it just in time to get through. James and the girls only had about a day left until the hallow tree locked them out for six months.

"Almost there," said James as the girls scuffled behind him. The three arrived in a cleared area with a gigantic stone statue of a Vonkern holding up a medieval-looking torch. "Wow!

That's neat!" said Anne. "Now, one of you needs to climb up that statue (which was about twenty feet tall) and light a fire." Why?" asked Nieve.

"Oh, you'll see," said James with a smirk. Anne, being a go-getter, decided she wanted to climb up the statue and light the fire. Clink, clink, scrape.

"There," said Anne. She lit the torch, and a green fire appeared which anyone could see for miles. "Now, close your eyes and whatever happens, don't come off that statue and lift your hands up as high as you can!" shouted James from the feet of the statue.

(This was quite an entertaining sight as Anne was shaking like a leaf) All of a sudden, what looked like a mini tornado appeared right above Anne and sucked her in. "Bam! Anne was gone! As though swallowed in midair. Then the fire gave out. "Oh my God!

screamed Nieve. "What just happened?" She cried. "Bahahaha! Laughed James in amusement as though he just saw an impressive performance.

"She's fine," he chuckled.

"This is a short cut to get us to the Hallow tree faster he said. "Come on, let us go," said James as he began to climb up the statue, "Okay," said Nieve.

The two climbed up the statue, Nieve lit the green fire, and the two raised their hands up to the sky as they smiled at each other.

Poof! Out they flew like helpless squirrels tossed by a catapult into a long waterfall heading towards a large light pink lake inside a cave (It was the cave with the hallow tree) at the bottom of the waterfall. Anne had been floating around practicing her backstrokes and grimacing.

"That was fun," said Anne, behaving as though she was living in a dream. "She gulped down some of the clear, refreshing water. It was so cool and refreshing after hours of traveling here and there since their entrance into the world. "Yes, it is" Agreed James and Nieve nodding their soaked heads in agreement as they began to join Anne in her floating and staring at the cave ceiling. The three took turns sipping the cool water from the lake and floating around belly up like happy frogs. "We have a few hours before we contin-ue on our way," said James as he smiled in a daze.

DARK WARLOCKS

"Nothing yet," said the dark warlock as he morphed back into his evil human form. Rezin was his name. He was on a mission to find the princesses, assigned by the witch since she heard rumors that they had come into the Petrified Kingdom of the Gourges.

Rezin was the witch's most trusted warlock. Rezin was like what Joseph Goebbels was to Adolph Hitler. He was the barge hound who was trying to pick up the girls' scent earlier in the story.

The witch had returned to her old quarters beyond the Frozen Mountains after she had cast her last spell (the special spell in liq-uid form which had put everyone to sleep so she could kidnap the King) in the Kingdom of the Endless Mountains. "Oh, memories" sighed the witch as she looked around in her old childhood home and breathed in lifeless, long unvisited air. The witch had grown up in an old wooden cottage, made of ancient black oak trees and clay. It was a humble cottage; it was only one floor with an attic which was her room as a child. The witch had not been home since she was a young girl — the weather in the area where the witch's childhood home was always snowing and strange. The snow would not pile up even though it was constantly snowing. The temperature would change slightly, but the snow was constant. At times, the snow would melt a little, then pile up a little but would never fully melt away or ever get past four feet of snow. It was though the land was cursed. Maybe, it was. "You were successful?" asked Rezin regarding the capture of the King as he interrupted the witch's thoughts (she was wondering why she had been born so ugly) while she was dwelling in self-pity as she was gazing sadly around at the snow which was falling. (They were not yet aware that the great Wizard Venton had rescued the King from her other home in our world.)

"Yes," said the witch nearly whispering as Rezin could see her breath. "The old fool is chasing around a deer! Ha! Haa" She scoffed with pride (as if she had won a prize). "I think the girls were spotted before us," said Rezin with concern.

"We shall raise the other warlocks then," said the witch with ambition as she swept her hideous corned foot across the snow-covered ground. (Rezin and the witch were going to prepare a spell to raise the dead warlocks from ancient times so that then they could raise a long, dead, and forgotten army).

REUNITED

"My babies!" Squealed Samara in delight as if she had seen the Easter bunny. Samara hugged her sisters. "You made it! Thank the waters!" said Petry gleefully. "Yes, thank the waters!" (That was a saying in the other world like ours when we say thank God) Said Joseph. James and the girls had finally arrived in the land of the Vonkerns, (after they had grown tired of swimming that is and Anne had mastered her backstroke). "How were your travels, brother? Were you followed?" asked Joseph. "Come here, brother" whispered James as he pulled Joseph aside and he handed him something covered in cloth. "What is this? Whispered Joseph "Shhh, shhh just open it and look" Muttered James as he pushed Joseph into the back room of Petry's house. "I don't want Petry to see," said James.

Many, many years ago, Petry suffered an attack by a barge hound. It was a horrific event. One day, Petry had been out minding his own business when quickly, something jumped him.

Since that incident, Petry had become so unusually paranoid. There were times where he would spontaneously wet himself from fear and have nervous breakdowns. Petry was always in his house early and tried to avoid going out alone whenever he could avoid it. Joseph, who often would visit Petry, chased the barge hound off. "Ohhh no!" Whispered Joseph as he looked horrified at what was in the cloth. The girls and Petry were now sitting around the fire, eating baked mushrooms, and giggling with Petry as they took turns pouring each other red flower tea. Red flower tea is extract from a flower, found only in the Vonkerns pine forest. The flower looked like a tiny pine tree as well but bloomed large red beautiful flowers and grew no more than a foot from the ground. The extract from the red flower was thick and sweet like honey and somehow brewed into the lands most comforting beverage. It was the most delicious thing someone who had been standing out in wintry weather would want to have and so soothing to the stomach. "We are waiting still on the bird," said Petry as he joined Joseph and James in the back room. (The girls were dosing off on blankets made by black camel fur in front of the fire).

Petry and Joseph had been waiting on the night bird (that belonged to the wizard Venton) to arrive to let them know if the wizard had found the King. The night birds were unique and highly intelligent birds and spoke in a coded chirping language which the Vonkerns had learned from being around them for so long.

It was much like our Morse code. The Wizard Venton's bird had been the first witness to the girls' arrival and had notified the wizard first and had been flying back and forth between the wizard and Petry communicating this entire time about the girls and the barge hound. Now, Petry had been waiting for the bird to return to him again about the whereabouts of the King.

MOTHER

"There was snow everywhere, Anne could feel the cold in her bones as she walked along the path while her teeth were jittering.

Anne could hear distant singing coming from a young child's voice. The melody was soft and sounded a bit sad. "Strange," thought Anne. "I don't recall being here, but it feels familiar" Anne thought to herself. Anne continued walking now up a steep hill then finally a small cozy cottage and in front of the house a small figure of a girl in a white hooded cloak. Anne noticed no one else around her, but the young girl who seemed to be drawing something on the snow-covered ground with a twig. "Hello!" Hello! Screamed Anne trying to get the young girl's attention. Suddenly, in less than a second, the girl in the cloak was right in front of her. "Hi! said the girl in a frightening voice and scaring Anne as she raised her face to her. Anne felt the most horrific chill down her spine and felt as though her stomach had fallen out of her. Anne noticed that the girl was faceless! "Ahhhhhh!" screamed Anne as she sat up.

It was a nightmare; she looked around and noticed Nieve and Samara lying on the floor near the almost vanished fire that was in the Vonkerns house. "What did you dream?" Whispered Joseph, who had been watching Anne sleep the entire time. "I saw a faceless girl in a white cloak," said Anne.

"Hmmm thought Joseph. "I wonder," said Joseph in his warm, comforting voice.

Joseph was the older of the brothers and more responsible. He was a more serious gourge than his younger brother James. James was the more mischievous of the two, and when he was younger, he was always getting into trouble and punished by his mother.

Once, James farted in a jar and then opened it in front of a girl's face just because he did not like her and then later, he nailed her with a rock right between the eyes. James was genuinely like Dennis the Menace. "Tell me, Anne," said Joseph. "What do you know about your mother?"

THE KING RETURNS

"Your Majesty!" Your Majesty!" Slap!

The wizard Venton smacked the King right in the face. "Your Majesty!!!" It had been hours since the Wizard Venton had transformed the King into a dwarf. It would only be temporary though since the witch's original spell had not broken yet.

The wizard now had to recast a spell on the King every twelve hours since the King would always turn back into a slow-minded vampire. The King was still in need of the witch's blood and the blood of a white witch to become human again permanently. In the meantime, the wizard thought it was better for the King to be a dwarf rather than a semi changed gourge. "Huh?" Muttered the now dwarf King. "Where am I?" asked the King as he began to sit up from the Wizards' uncomfortable straw bed filled with hay and small insects. "You're in the Kingdom of the Mythical Valley, your highness," said the wizard looking quite worried. "You are in my home. "said the wizard. "What am I doing here??" said the King in a voice that sounded like he had been sucking helium. "Ohhhhh!

"Just a moment your highness," said the wizard as the dwarf spell was beginning to wear off and the King's skin was beginning to change again turning back into a semi gourge. "Ahhh!" Whimpered the King pitifully as he saw he was changing. "Help me! "cried the hopeless King. "Be still and shut up!" said the wizard, annoyed by the King's cries. "Aledabayah ... baaaabdoooie goo mooshkaaah!" said the wizard as he waved his wonderful green wand over the King, preventing him from becoming a semi-gourge. "Poof!" The King was a dwarf again. "What's going on??" asked the King angrily. "The witch put a curse on you; your majesty" Explained the wizard.

"She has disguised herself as an old lady and fooled you, then she made herself to look like you and has tried to turn our Kingdoms against each other"

TRAPPED

"I hope we make it," said Sir Vallah to the night bird. The Knight climbed up on the Statue (The same statue that James and the girls had traveled to get to the Land of the Vonkerns) The Knight lit a fire in the torch and held up the bird as high as he could and poof! Out they flew and landed in the pink water where James and the girls had previously been practicing their backstrokes. "Oh, this is good water," said Sir Vallah through is curly red beard as he tasted the pink water in the cave. (He was the same knight that had gone with the wizard in rescuing the King earlier).

When the wizard had rescued the King, he sent the night bird and Sir Vallah off to the Land of the Vonkerns to try and warn James and Joseph about the barge hound that the night bird had noticed when it was flying around trying to find the girls. Unfortunately, the way to the World Beneath (the land of the Vonkerns) closed, and now they would have to wait six months in the cave. Sir Vallah and the night bird became trapped inside the cave.

STEW

"What else shall I fetch?" asked Rezin, "I need a heart of a red fairy," said the witch. "It is back in my other home where my children have grown," said the witch. "I have it locked away in my cupboard in an old jar," said the witch. "I shall go and get it," said Rezin. (Meanwhile, Sir Vallah and the night bird were taking a nap on their backs in the cave dreaming of wonderful bunnies and fairies) "That won't be necessary," said the witch. "Instead, there are red fairies in the frozen mountains; you can find them at the top; it is only a few hours travel," said the witch. "Yes, mam," said Rezin as he began to morph back into a barge hound and head out of the witch's home.

A WALK IN THE NIGHT

"Not much," said Anne. "I only know what my father has told me," said Anne to Joseph. "And what is that?" asked Joseph, "Umm, that she was a strange woman and she died of an illness," said Anne. "Come, let us take a walk," said Joseph as he led Anne out of Petry's home. It was a beautiful night as always in that land of

the Vonkerns. Anne and Joseph began to walk down a path behind Petry's house.

Anne and her sisters did not know that their mother had been a
beautiful white witch, and that was the reason that they had such
odd dreams.

THE MERMAID-LIKE CREATURES

"You will be safe here my future King," said the mermaid-like creature in a cool calm voice as it slithered back into the green Seas of
Neros. Prince Shabah of the Kingdom of the Mythical Valley (The
Prince who King Giorgio had arranged for his daughter Nieve to
marry) had been evacuated to safety into the Seas of Neros, (which
is southeast of the land of the Vonkerns) when his highest-ranking
Knights had received news from the Wizard Venton's night bird
that his future father in law, King Giorgio, had been abducted. The
Wizard Venton, (who was King Shabah's father) lost no time in ar-
ranging a haven for his son.

Many years ago, when the Great Wizard Venton was a young apprentice under the teachings of a great spell knower, he had met a
beautiful young lady who unknown to the apprentice Venton, was
the future wife of the King of the Mythical Valley. Soon after the
young lad wed the King and gave birth to the apprentice's son , she

and the Wizard Venton agreed to keep their son a secret and allow the King to raise the child as his own on the promise that she would find a way to keep the wizard in the castle so he could be close to his son and so when the King of the Mythical Valley was seeking an advisor to assist in decisions with the Kingdom, his wife recommended the Wizard Venton to him and that is how the Wizard Venton came to work in the castle as the King's great Advisor and caretaker of the Prince of the Mythical Valley.

STUCK IN PARADISE

"What shall we do now?" asked Sir Vallah.

It had been the night bird and Sir Vallah's one-hundredth time playing hide and seek in the cave where they were trapped for some time now since the hole at the base of the hollow tree had closed on them. Poor Sir Vallah's beard had grown to his belly now, and his belly was now shrinking since he was now on a diet of fish and hallow tree fruit. "Amazing," said Sir Vallah. "I can see my toes now since I've lost weight," said the red-headed Knight. Imagine a scrawny redheaded homeless man, but with medieval attire on, that is now how poor Sir Vallah had come to look like, and he smelled of fish. " Oooh, what I would do for a cup of tasty mint ale right now" whispered the Knight. "There must be another way out of here," he grumbled miserably.

"Chirp" chirped the night bird. "Great idea," said the Knight. Sir Vallah and the night bird agreed that the night bird would peck his way out of the cave, they might as well since there was nothing better to do, they were stuck in the cave for about a month now, and it was another five months before the hole would open again. Away pecked the night bird at the speed of a turtle.

CONTINUING THE WALK...

"Your mother was a white witch," said Joseph.

Anne gasp in disbelief. "What?

How?" questioned Anne. Joseph and Anne had now arrived on the beach behind the pine forest behind Petry's house. I can see your mother in you said Joseph as he stared at Anne sadly. A long time ago, Joseph had loved Anne's mother in another life it seemed. Anne's mother, Penelope, knew of her coming death when the girls were young, and so she put a magic spell on herself so that at the time of her death her soul would split into two souls and merge with the souls of her daughters so that she could be with them throughout their lives literally living inside of them and guiding them.

"Your mother was very graceful, and I see her in you and your sisters," said Joseph. On the night that Penelope had died she had spent her entire last day with her girls, she had taken them swimming in the Depths of Neros with the mermaids and on that evening when she had laid her girls to sleep peacefully she snuck out into the waters and peacefully drowned herself so that she could die her own way and not the way that she had foreseen. Joseph was remembering Penelope when she had passed, for he had been the one to find her body on the beach when the Sea's had given her up. Penelope had been Joseph's first love when they were children, but over time they grew apart and went their separate ways. Joseph and Penelope had stayed good friends, but deep down, although Penelope fell in love with the King and married him, Joseph had still loved her in his heart.

As they continued to walk, Joseph remembered the smell of her hair. "What is that?" asked Anne, pointing out to the water. Across the water Anne and Joseph saw a figure of light that looked like a woman wearing a long elegant dress and flowing golden hair walking on the water, "Anne" said the figure faintly" the womanly figure glowed in a dim blue color as it began to approach them. "Mom"? said Anne in total shock.

"Yes, it's me said Penelope's soul.

FUNERAL

"He was my companion" cried the Wizard Venton.

The wizard and a few of his friends had a funeral for his night bird since he had been missing for over a month all assumed that he had died. (meanwhile, the poor bird was still pecking away at the cave walls where he and Sir Vallah were in) "May he rest in peace" said the Montrale Monk. The Montrale Monk was a Monk from a land of pyramids deep in a jungle found in the east part of the Mythical Valley. The pyramids were much like the Aztec pyramids in Mexico.

The Mythical Valley was mysterious, indeed. Half the land in the Mythical Valley was in a slight fog where the hidden pyramids were at.

In the center of the Mythical Valley was a large, calm red sea-like lake. In the center of the lake was an island with creatures, unlike any place you could find since the creatures had been isolated. The creatures on the island were unique because of how they evolved to adapt to their environment. In the summer months above the sea-like lake appeared lights much like our northern lights in Alaska. To put things into perspective, the Mythical Valley was the size of our Africa.

CHAPTER 3

"Up you fool!" cried the witch. "Up!!" Rezin and the witch had completed casting the spell to raise the dead warlocks from their graves. "We have much to do," said the witch. "They are like infants, so helpless!" complained the witch. The witch and Rezin had gone to a forgotten place.

They were in an old ancient battlefield where a long, forgotten war had taken place a long time ago where the witch's father had died. Many lives were lost at this war, and it was so intense. It was a war where many wizards and dragons (the dragons almost became extinct because of the war) had died along with many of the ancestors of the other Kingdoms before the witch had put her filthy curse upon The Kingdom of Stone, now known as The Kingdom of the Gourges or The Petrified Kingdom before it had been cursed. The witch remembered the day of the battle.

Abigail (the witch) was just a child when her father, who had become a dark warlock, decided to launch a war with the King (King Giorgio's father) of the Kingdom of Stone.

STRANDED

"Now what?" sighed Sir Vallah.

The night bird and Sir Vallah had finally escaped from the cave and entered the World of the Vonkerns (or so they thought) but unfortunately for them, when they entered what they thought was the World Beneath it didn't happen to be right in the forest on land like mostly everybody usually arrived, with their luck, they landed right in the center of what looked like a red sea on some kind of island (they didn't know they were on an island) The two were starving and quickly built a fire and began to explore around the island to look for food. What happened to the bird and Sir Vallah, is that they were fooled into going into the Mythical Valley.

Someone or something with extreme powerful magic had intercepted them when they jumped into the hole at the hallow tree and sent them straight into the Mythical Valley.

THE TRUTH

"It is time," said Joseph as he stood in front of the girls with Petry and James. "You know what will happen when we do this," said Petry.

"Yes, said Joseph. "I will take them afterward to the place once this is complete," said James. "Agreed brother," said Joseph. It was now early morning, and all three sisters were going to take another trip to another unknown place led by James. "We shall meet him there when we arrive," said James as he bade farewell to his brother Joseph as he left him behind with Petry. On a boat they went, the girls and James. It was a large boat which looked much like our boats from the seventeen hundreds in our world. It was black and had sails over thirty feet high, and the girls were excited for they had never been on a boat ride. "Where are we going" asked Samara. "I can't tell you," said James. "It is for your own safety," he lied.

Meanwhile, as Samara and James were chatting away, Anne had isolated herself while still trying to process everything she had learned from the night before when she and Joseph had seen her mother's soul on the beach.

What happened was that Anne learned the truth. Penelope's soul or ghost, whatever it was, showed Anne through like a vision of sorts what had really happened in the past before she was born. It was like watching a movie and being in it at the same time, in a way, it was as though Anne had traveled through time. Anne was shown the ancient battle that happened between the witch's father, Agarion. Agarion was King Giorgio's stepbrother. It was all beginning to make sense now. King Melagolin (King Giorgio's stepfather) had banished Agarion when he discovered that his son who was next in line to rule the Kingdom of Stone (the Petrified Kingdom) had decided to turn into a warlock. Magic was a thing that had run through the veins of the royal family of the Kingdom of

Stone for centuries. Magic was not a gift that everyone had owned, especially magic as strong as theirs.

There was a rule which was never to be broken, if you were a royal, and that rule was never to practice black magic. So long as you were part of the royal family, you had to stay pure and good, and Agarion had long strayed from good. King Melagolin removed his first-born son's place from being next in line for King and banished him from the Kingdom of Stone sending him far into the mountains, which had become the witch's home, and forbade him from ever returning. Agarion grew resentful and more powerful in dark magic, then he tried to gather an army against his father but failed. That was the battle against Agarion where both father and son died, but Giorgio remained alive and took Agarion's place as King.

Agarion's children, Alexander and Abigail were looked after by Rezin, who was Agarion's best friend and who had also taught Agarion about dark magic.

SECRETS OF THE PAST

There was another secret from the past that few knew about. During the battle of Agarion when dragons were abundant, King Melagolin commanded his knights to take some of the dragons to the Seas of Neros; the King knew that his son would try to destroy all the dragons since they were the best weapons in war and their blood was sacred. The King's best wizard developed a strong potion that would transform the dragons into something else to hide them. The dragons were turned into mermaids, the mermaids in the Seas of Neros.

THEY'RE ALIVE

"They're alive!" cried the wizard! "Thank the heavens! They're alive!" he said. "They are in the Jungles of the Mythical Valley," said Sir Harrist. "Sir Harrist had seen Sir Vallah and the Wizard's night bird wandering lost and confused in the Jungles in the Mythical Valley. "We must go to them," said the Wizard Venton. "As you wish, old wise one said Sir Harrist as he bowed before the wizard" Suddenly Sir Harrist began to glow green and transformed into his true self. Sir Harrist was a dragon, but not just any dragon.

Sir Harrist was really *Trimbass the Black*!

Trimbass the Black was the Ruler of all the dragons that had fought in the Battle of Agarion. He was the biggest and oldest dragon that ever existed, his wingspan was fifty feet, and his breath was hot like fire. Trimbass's eyes resembled green fire, and his skin was entirely black and as hard as pure diamond. Trimbass had given King Melagolin permission to transform all the other dragons into mermaids to hide them from extinction until the time was right.

Trimbass the Black lowered his wing allowing the wizard to climb onto his back and off they flew to the Mythical Valley.

BACK ON THE BOAT

"Are we there yet?

"Moaned Nieve. "I'm sick of eating fish," she said. "It's good for you," said James as he was daydreaming by the edge of the boat. James was recalling the young girl who he had hit with a rock between the eyes when he was much younger and how she had dizzy spells for some time after. "Heh, heh" He chuckled as he looked like a crazy man with schizophrenia from the girl's perspective. "You're so weird," said Anne, "Uuuugh," said Nieve. The girls and James had been at sea for what seemed like years. By now they had all finally grown used to the movement of the boat and no longer vomited like they did at first. James had also made it his duty to get the girls in top physical shape before arriving to their destination. The girls had to swim several laps to and from the boat daily and catch their own fish if they wanted to eat. The girls' sense of direction was perfected. They all knew exactly which direction was north and learned all the constellations in the sky.

They really were not all too far from their destination now, but James did not tell them that. For the past, few weeks James was sending the boat in circles to delay their arrival just to make sure he had trained the girls just the way he wanted. "We are almost there," said James to the exasperated girls as they were finishing their laps to and from the boat. "Finally!!!" Shouted Anne as she was spitting nasty seawater infested with fish pee. "I can't wait!" said Samara.

IN THE JUNGLE

"I think we have been here before" Stated the exhausted Sir Vallah. "Chirpity chirp" Peeped the night bird. It was a humid day in the Mythical Valley. "I'm certain we went through the hallow tree, and these trees are not the same... the species looks different" muttered Sir Vallah.

The Night bird and Sir Vallah had been wandering lost and confused through the Mythical Valley for days now.

It was humid and filled with insects and nothing like the land of the Vonkerns. There was no beautiful scent of the woods, and the two were sore and thirsty. "I'm starved!" said the hungry Knight. "Let us take a break and eat," said Sir Vallah. "I'll start the fire, and you get the spices," said Sir Vallah to the Night bird" The

Night bird flew off into the sky and began picking off different leaves from trees for spices while the Knight began to start a fire.

BASHEMDAR

"It's him!" I know it!" Exclaimed the Great Wizard Venton. "There was nothing I could do!" said the terrified wizard. "I am nothing, but a glorified magician compared to him!" mumbled Venton. "But how is that possible?" asked King Giorgio. "I don't know your majesty, but I know it's him" Uttered the magus. "We shall have a meeting then," said the King.

"When my daughters arrive, we shall continue with the plan that the Vonkern and the others have decided and then once we are all well again, we shall all gather at the old meeting place where my father and our fathers before us made the great decisions. "The curse that the old hag placed on me may have been a blessing in disguise" Suggested the King. "As you wish," said the Wizard Venton. "I shall gather the birds to send off your message," Stated Venton.

What had occurred was that when the wizard and Sir Harrist, (Trimbass the Black) had flown to recover the Knight and the Night bird, they had grown weak and unable to continue flying. They began to walk through the jungles, and as they walked, they began to recognize that they were developing symptoms from an old type of magic which could only come from a long, forgotten, enemy of theirs. This enemy had committed a terrible crime against the dragons and the old dead King Melagolin. Bashemdar was the evil creature's name. Bashemdar tried to get close to the King Melagolin to try and achieve power, but some of the King's advisers and Knights did not trust Bashemdar. When Bashemdar realized he would never have a position of power, he slaughtered a dragon and drank its sacred blood. When Bashemdar drank the blood of the dragon it strengthened his magic, but at the same time since the dragon had not given him his blood willingly, the blood became cursed and so Bashemdar became cursed as well.

HEART OF THE UNKNOWN SEA

"We have arrived!! Exclaimed the gourge James with his usual smile. "Oh finally," said Anne. "For real this time?" asked Nieve. For on their way, James had been cruelly pranking the girls of their arrival.

James would wait until they were asleep or calm and suddenly exclaim to the girls that they had arrived when they had not. "Welcome," said a Montrale monk respectfully. "It is a pleasure and a relief to have you here said another Monk. The Montrale monks were intimidating, human-like creatures, their eyes were silver in color, and their pupils were too dark to see. When speaking to a Montrale monk, they lacked most expression, and you could never really tell how one was feeling unless he told you how he was feeling.

The Montrale monks were longtime friends of the Vonkerns, and in the Heart of the Unknown Sea, the Vonkerns and the Monks lived together in harmony. The Heart of the Unknown Sea was to the right of the World Beneath and below the Mythical Valley, it was hidden and traveled from the Mythical Valley.

The Heart of the Unknown Sea was an island that drifted apart from The World beneath (Land of the Vonkerns), and the waters that were between the Heart of the Unknown Sea and the Mythical Valley were too dangerous to sail from and so the only way to get to The Heart of the Unknown Sea was by sailing from the Land of the Vonkerns.

LIFTING THE CURSE

"I found it," said Petry.

Petry and the gourge Joseph had traveled to the Kingdom of the Endless Mountains to find the piece of flesh that King Giorgio had bitten off the witch when she had kidnapped him and taken him to her human home. The Wizard Venton had retrieved the flesh from the King's mouth, which held some blood from the witch (which was needed to lift the curse that was placed on the Old Petrified Kingdom) and placed it in a jar and hid it inside one of his homes. The Wizard Venton had many homes since he enjoyed traveling to so many various places. "What a place for a great wizard!" said Joseph looking around Venton's home with disgust. "You would think that with all his herbs and books he would be more organized," said Joseph disappointed at the Wizards mess. "Hmm, what is this," said Petry with much curiosity. "Don't touch anything said Joseph" "Ah! Ah! chooo!" Sneezed Petry as a blue sparkly powder blue onto Joseph. "Oh! What have you done?!!," cried Joseph. Joseph had shrunk to a foot tall. "Your adorable exclaimed Petry rather proud of himself" "I'm going to kill you!!" Howled Joseph as he looked at himself in a mirror in horror and then growled viciously at Petry. Joseph who could be mistaken as a cat or small dog if you did not know any better, except he walked upright and had a sword. "We must get on with our task," said Petry" Hop on!" he said. Joseph then, like a small child, hopped onto Petry's back and wrapped his furry arms around Petry's neck then off they went with the flesh in a jar to meet with the Wizard Venton.

WHO IS REZIN?

"I have them lost and confused," said Rezin. "Soon we shall both have our revenge," said the witch.

"I will get the armies ready, and you bring the Knight and the old bird here" Clucked the witch. Unknown to the witch and many others, Rezin was Bashemdar.

"As you wish my lady," said Bashemdar in a dark, mysterious voice.

"But first, I must kill you," Laughed Bashemdar.

"Whaaaat?! asked the surprised witch.

"You are but a lowly wizard," she said in her insulted voice as she looked coldly at who she thought was Rezin, the wizard. "How dare you threaten me!!" said the witch. "You see, my lady," said Bashemdar. I am not just a lowly wizard; I am Bashemdar!" Buahahahahaaa!! He laughed.

"It was I who turned your father Agarion against your grandfather King Melagolin" Hissed Bashemdar. "Your stinky rotten grandfather refused to promote me in his worthless Kingdom!! Snickered Bashemdar. "But you died!" whimpered the witch. "That wasn't me who died," said Bashemdar. "That was your mother!" Stated Bashemdar. "I had your mother drink one of my potions, and it transformed her into my twin" Snickered Bashemdar. "Your own father killed your mother in battle thinking it was me," said Bashemdar. "And now you shall die!!" squealed Bashemdar in intense joy. "But why?" cried the witch. "Why kill me?" whimpered Abigail. "Because as long as you live, the curse can be lifted said Bashemdar. "And I have *never* liked your family," said Bashemdar.

THE GATHERING

"Ahh! You found it!

Said the wizard. "Good let us get started then shall we" he said. Petry handed the wizard the jar with the piece of flesh in it" "Oh my!" said Venton. "I thought I got rid of that old fairy powder!" He exclaimed while staring at poor shrunken Joseph. "Well, once this is complete, it should help with your height as well," he said to Joseph.

The wizard dropped the piece of flesh into a mixture of unknown magical ingredients inside a large black cauldron and began to stir it while chanting something in a strange unknown wizard language which sounded like a dialect of French and Arabic. It was an ancient wizard language which passed on from generations of wizards. A thick fog began to pour out from the cauldron and spread all over the room.

Soon, the fog became so large it started spreading outside of the castle through the windows and under the doors.

"Here said Venton to Joseph as he handed him a cup of the mixture" All you need is a sip" "Thank you," said Joseph as he sipped the cup.

"Now, to make things quicker let's pour some in the waters so that everyone who is cursed can have a drink." The wizard and the others who were with him began to pour the cure into the lakes and rivers of the local land, and all those afflicted by the witch's horrible invocation began to change back into their formal selves.

"Your Majesty, good to have you back to your old self," said the wizard as he glanced at King Giorgio. "It's good to be back," said the King. Now, let us have our great assembly," said the King in a more confident voice than before.

THE DOOR

It was deep within the waters between the Heart of the Unknown Sea and the Mythical Valley. It was a door locked long ago, which was holding back a secret. It was a secret that no living soul wanted to uncover.

The presence of this locked up secret had tainted the waters and the skies that surrounded the door. The once calm and clear sea became dark red and corrupt.

Many of the sea life that used to exist in those waters fled or died. The passage once used to travel closed off. Pirates and traders would get lost and go missing when they tried to sail across the waters.

THE GREAT DECISION

"Are we all here now?" asked James. "Yes, we are all here now," said Prince Shabah. All the Kings, the King's advisors, and wise necromancers from all the lands had finally gathered together in the old decision room where many Rulers from the past had gathered together from different lands to discuss and decide important things and politics. "Ring the bell and lock the doors," said someone from the crowd. The ringing of the bell had been a custom that was passed on from long ago.

Once the bell was rung, no one inside the decision room could leave, and no one from outside the decision room could disturb those inside. "So, let us begin," said Aptos, the leader of the

Vonkerns. "If we are to unlock the door, how are we go beneath the waters?" he asked. "We can try using a mermaid!" shouted an adviser. "But the waters are cursed," said another. "Are there any spells that can protect the mermaids?" asked a different creature. And so, the debate continued.

SMOKEY FIRE

"There was fire everywhere, and the smell of burning hair filled the Knight's nostrils as he lifted himself from the ground. It was dark out, and he could not see a living thing anywhere in sight. "Over here," said a voice. The Knight glanced and squinted his eyes, and there in the trees, he saw what looked like a green fire-fly" Come" said the voice" The Knight stood up with his sword still at his side and began to walk into the woods. As he walked, he could hear the breaking of twigs and grass, suddenly there in front of him was a snake. The snake was giant in size, and it was crouched down behind some bushes. "Don't be afraid," hissed the snake.

The snake then opened its large jaws and jumped towards the Knight, biting his head. "Ahhh!" screamed the Knight as he fell over onto the floor.

"Huh," said the Knight. Sir Vallah was in a cell of some sort, and there in the corner of the cell was the night bird lying motionless but breathing.

"Sleep good?" asked someone.

"Where am I?" asked Sir Vallah.

"Oh, don't worry, said the voice.

"Your somewhere safe and far too.

Far from everything where no one can ever find you," Snickered the voice. "Here, I need you alive," said the voice as someone or something slid a tray food from beneath the door.

DEFEATED

Down she went into the snow in a valley deep inside the frozen mountains. She was exhausted and tired and had not eaten since she escaped. It was the witch. Abigail had barely escaped her death from Bashemdar. "Monster!" she claimed to herself as she limped through the snow. "To think I thought of him as family" She muttered as though she had had her heartbroken from a long, frustrating relationship. "I will get him back," said the witch. "My poor mother!" she cried. "I will avenge my mother," she said to herself.

ZIDUS

"Lock the door! Quickly!" he said. Zidus went through the colossal door. He had taken the bait. "Victory" cried the Vonkerns and the Monks. "Victory!" They shouted and cheered as they all raised their arms. Suddenly the skies darkened, and the ships were beginning to rock back and forth as the waters began to change beneath them, and the wind began to pick up with a scent of evil. "Sail away! Sail away," cried a pirate. "He is going to curse us!" The Vonkerns and the Monks turned their ships and began to sail away. Some sailed towards the World Beneath and others tried to sail back to The Mythical Valley. The Vonkerns and the Monks had succeeded in capturing the mammoth God-like creature that had been tormenting them. It was the last of the Sekhemets to finally be locked away. The Sekhemets were creatures that did not belong to the land they were tormenting, at least that is what some thought. No one knew where the Sekhemets came from or when they came. Some believed they had always been here, and others thought they arrived from somewhere else. There were even some who thought they were Gods that deserved worship. Whatever the Sekhemets were, they did not seem pleased. "Let the waters fall!! Drop the waters," cried a monk to the Enchanter.

The Enchanter then signaled to the other warlocks to let the waters fall back into the sea where they had come and buried the door with the ocean to make sure Zidus would not come out ever again.

THE GOAT

"Baaaa!

Baaa!" said Abigail. The witch had turned herself into a goat. She was fearful of discovery, and so as she was wandering through

woods after she escaped from her death, she decided she would go incognito as a goat. Who would ever suspect a goat to ever be a witch and a goat was quite a common creature too? The witch had been suffering from severe identity problems after she discovered who Rezin really was and how he had killed her mother. Abigail would cry herself at night for she felt lonely, afraid, and abandoned. She also decided to transform her beautiful self (at least *she* thought she was beautiful there were others who thought differently) into a goat since as a goat she could eat anything and did not need shelter to stay warm in freezing weather. The witch was not really a good artisan, and she just thought it would be more logical to change herself into an animal that could sustain itself better than a helpless human who did not know how to build a house. "Mabey I should become a white witch," thought Abigail" "Hmm" she pondered as she began to munch on some plants.

139

CHAPTER 4

"How is their training coming along," asked Bashemdar. "They are developing well overall, but some have forgotten many of the spells. One of the warlocks tried to transform another warlock into a dragon, but instead he became a chicken," said a servant. Bashemdar had taken over the witch's old home and created a fortress to prepare the army of warlocks that he and the witch had risen. He wanted to bring war against all the Kingdoms and Rule over everyone and everything. (The fortress looked much like the Rumeli Fortress in Turkey.) "And what about the Knight?" asked Bashemdar. Bashemdar's slaves had captured the Knight and were interrogating him about the location of something extremely important. What occurred long ago when Zidus, locked away behind the door beneath the waters, the key used to lock the door was put away in a secret place so that no one could ever free Zidus again. Sir Vallah was the only known person who knew where the key hid and so that is why Bashemdar wanted him. "Keep examining him" voiced Bashemdar.

THE ANSWER

"We have made our decision," said Aptos. After much debate, the meeting was finally over. The Kingdoms would split and go on three separate missions. One Kingdom would go on a rescue mission to retrieve Sir Vallah another would sail out and protect the door from anyone trying to cross over the waters from the Mythical Valley and the last Kingdom was going to protect the girls. "The Mythical Valley is proper," said King Giorgio as he bade farewell to his daughters. He had decided since he was going to wed his daughter Nieve to The King of the Mythical Valley it only made sense to send his daughters there. Once the girls arrived in the Kingdom of the Mythical Valley, Nieve's wedding would take place to finally unite the Kingdoms as one.

BUTTINSKY

"Here, Buttinsky. Here girl" said a boy. Ascot was his name. One evening when Ascot was doing his daily chore of gathering firewood, he noticed something in the wood. When he went to investigate, he found a black and white goat eating away. Ascot instantly fell in love with the goat and brought her to his home where he decided to name her Buttinsky. Unknown to him, he had brought home a witch. The witch had been stalking the family from the woods for some time now and had been longing to sleep inside some type of dwelling for she was growing sick of the outdoors. The witch was still so fearful of detection since she had enemies everywhere and was not ready to turn back into human form. The witch just wanted to take a break after so many things had happened in her life and so she continued disguising herself as a harmless goat.

BACK TO THE BEGINNING

No one knew exactly when it happened. He had taken his sons and vanished. The man was strange and unaccepted, and everyone knew something would eventually happen. He was quite intelligent and beyond his time. After the loss of his wife, he was determined to get her back at whatever cost. He wanted the life he never had. Strange lights and sounds of explosions came from his house at all hours of the night. Henry, a great scientist, and genius discovered something extraordinary. Stories that he had discovered a link between time and magic spread. Others claimed he went insane and murdered his sons. Henry found a type of wormhole which one would expect to find in space.

What he found was something like another planet, but it was within our planet. Without much hesitation, Henry took his sons and explored the place. He had only gone a few times on his own without anyone's knowledge, and each time he stayed longer and longer until finally one day, he just didn't come back.

JAMES AND JOSEPH

Before I continue the story, I have not mentioned much about James and Joseph. What we know so far is that they are brothers and citizens of the Kingdom of Stone. Remember, the Kingdom of Stone was the Petrified Kingdom of the Gourges, but now that the curse lifted it became the Kingdom of Stone once again. So, anyway, James and Joseph were actually great leaders who had stayed behind when the family of white witches (King Giorgio had no magic blood in him which explains why he was not immune to the witch's curse earlier in the story, if you recall he had been adopted into the royal family by King Melagolin and taken Agarion's place) escaped through the portal and hid in the Kingdom of the Endless Mountains. Penelope, the girls' mother (through whom the girls' inherited their magic blood) had created the portal before she had died. She had suspected there would be a time when her daughters were going to need to escape.

The Kingdom of the Endless Mountains was supposed to be King Giorgio's Kingdom anyway before his father; King Melagolin passed away.

King Melagolin wanted to divide his kingdom between his two sons: Giorgio and Agarion who were about twenty years apart, Agarion being the oldest. During King Melagolin's reign the Kingdom of the Endless Mountains and the Kingdom of Stone were one single Kingdom under King Melagolin. Also, the reason the witch killed Penelope (who unknown to the witch Penelope was her aunt) was because she was trying to prevent any future attempts of lifting the curse which she was planning on the Kingdom. The witch and her brother Alexander were quite young when their father Agarion had died, and since their father was banished from the Kingdom of Stone by Melagolin, they never knew of their uncle Giorgio whose daughters were white witches. Sadly, once a white witch turns from good to evil, a curse placed on their future children passes on, which is why poor Abigail had been born so defected.

The curse is different for everyone, though, Abigail's brother was not hideous outwardly, but inwardly he was evil.

THE HUMAN KINGDOMS

The Kingdom of the Mythical Valley was the oldest of the Kingdoms. Humans were found only in the Kingdom of the Endless Mountains and the Kingdom of Stone apart from the Kingdom of the Mythical Valley (home of the Montrale Monks) whom they had agreed to stay separate but united through marriages. Therefore, Nieve had to marry Prince Shabah; had she refused to marry him a war would have started. The Vonkerns were mostly to themselves; they indulged with their baking and were closest to the Kingdom of the Mythical Valley. Now, what has become strange is that the humans in this world were not always in this world. If you remember the scientist, Henry had discovered a wormhole from the human world.

Henry and his sons were the first humans to enter the world, and from them, the human Kingdoms came to be.

JUST FELLOW WARLOCKS

Sir Harrist (Trimbass the Black) stayed behind as the others moved ahead with the plan. His job was to come in and aid as a last resort in case the other two failed in retrieving the Knight. "I will draw them out," said the wizard who decided to join King Giorgio's Knights. They had planned to disguise themselves as women in distress to draw out two warlocks from Bashemdar's fort so that they could steal their clothes and try and sneak in to retrieve Sir Vallah who was still suffering interrogation.

"Ready?" asked the wizard. "Ready," said the Knights" Poof! Venton smacked some special changing magic powders on the Knights, and they became dazzling damsels. "Ohhh! Ahhh! Help me!" cried one of the Knights. Venton was now pretending to choke one of the women and out came a warlock. "What kind of man chokes a woman!!" snarled the warlock. "Come Menengor" said the warlock to his friend who had followed behind him. "This magician here needs to be taught some manners."

Venton then vanished away into the woods, and as the two warlocks chased after him, the so-called women knocked them out unconscious and put their robes on. In they went into the fortress. Inside it was like a maze; the Knights moved swiftly with their heads lowered carefully avoiding recognition. Finally, they found the cell where Sir, Vallah, and the night bird were imprisoned. "Pssst!" Pssst!" said one of the Knights to Sir Vallah. "Huh," said Sir Vallah so skinny now his ribs were sticking out.

"We're rescuing you" said one of the Knights. "We must go this way," whispered Sir Vallah as the Knights began bending the bars with their swords freeing Sir Vallah. "Oh wait, we must get the bird," said Sir Vallah. He then went back into the cell, which was pitch black and accidentally stepped on the night bird. The bird let out a painful cry alerting their escape! "Don't let them get away!!,"cried a warlock. Out they ran as fast they could with the bird stuffed inside a pocket of one the robes and out, they fled meeting the wizard. The wizard let out a loud whistle and then Sir Harrist flew down and scooped them up flying back to the Kingdom of Stone.

QUEEN

The celebration was wonderful.

Nieve, who was now Queen and King Shabah were enjoying themselves. There were delicious baked mushrooms and music and performances all around them. The ground covered in flower petals and Vonkerns and humans alike were overjoyed and singing. "What a beautiful Queen we have," said one. "Much agreed," said someone else. Nieve's dress was long and elegant and a lovely shade of pink. Her crown was dazzling and fit perfectly upon her head. King Shabah had gifted her a small village in the Mythical Valley to name and rule as her own. "Mmmm," said Nieve. "This isn't so bad," she said as a Knight had offered her a taste of some mint ale" "I can teach you the recipe," said the proud Knight with a smile, overjoyed that the new Queen liked his beverage. "Come my dearest," said King Shabah warm as ever to his new bride as he took her over to meet a Vonkern" "For you, my Queen," said the Vonkern with a bow as he led a camel which was captured from the desert in the World Beneath to the Queen. "Oh my" Gasped Nieve. "He is tame, and you may ride him," said the Vonkern proudly. "Thank you," said the Queen as she began to pet the camel and thought of what to name it.

SHOULD WE?

"I think I know what it is," said Aptos. A group of the Vonkerns had volunteered with some Montrale Monks to go on the mission to protect the door where Zidus was kept. They were having second thoughts about guarding the door and opening it themselves. "It could kill Bashemdar. It might be our only chance," said a monk. They had heard from a night bird that there might be a way to control a Sekhemet. What many forgot about night birds is that these birds had a lifespan like a human if not longer. Petry had met a night bird once that claimed to be two hundred years old. Night birds had a long history of being popular pets among wizards and witches, and so many had knowledge of magic and secrets that others did not. "What else did the bird say?" said a Vonkern. "A necklace," said a Vonkern who was communicating with the bird. "The one wearing the necklace can control the Sekhemet," he said.

MEMORIES

"I love you too, mommy," said Abigail as she hugged her mother. "I have to go now, Abigail," said Lanesta. "Mommy, nooo!" "Baaaaa!!" said the witch as she awoke. She jumped up suddenly on all fours, terrified at her hoofs since she had forgotten she was still in goat form. "What is with that goat!" said a friend of the family looking suspiciously at Abigail, who had now been taken in

as a pet. "We think the poor animal was abused said Ascot's father (the father of the boy who had found Abigail). "She does act strange for a goat," said Ascot's mother. Abigail had a flashback of the last day she saw her mother. Lanesta had given Abigail a necklace. *"You'll know when to wear this," said Lanesta.* Remembered Abigail.

BACK HOME

"I need a vacation," said Sir Vallah. Venton, Sir Harrist (Trimbass the Black), the Night Bird, Sir Vallah and the two Knights that rescued Sir Vallah all arrived at the Kingdom of the Endless Mountains.

"Mooola, muska vaaaaheee...ere ....

wee!" said the wizard as he transformed the Knights who rescued Sir Vallah back into their manly selves. "Poof" They were men once again. "I never want to go through that again!" said one of the Knights. "Thank you for your help," said Venton as he bade the Knights farewell, releasing them back to their normal duties. "Oh, my poor friend," said the wizard as he held the night bird petting it as you would pet a cat. "It's good to see you alive," said Venton to the bird. The poor bird had lost some of his feathers and a bit of weight.

LIGHTS IN THE SKY

There were lights in the sky, and comets were shooting down fast. There were eruptions around, and the Kingdom was on fire. Nieve and Anne lied motionless on the ground covered in cinders and smoke was everywhere. Samara was in shock, not knowing what to do. Samara just stood there covered in ashes as she gawked at everything that was happening around her. "Samara," said a voice. Samara turned around "Samara," said the voice again. Samara woke up. It was dead night, and she could see light outside the castle window. "Samara' whispered someone again. Samara gasped. She looked around the room and noticed light coming from the foyer. Samara quietly began to walk out of the bedroom into the hallway. Down the hallway, she noticed an obscure figure that walked down some stairs. "Samara," she heard. The Princess then decided not to follow the voice and went back into the room and bolted the door shut. Samara jumped backed onto the bed under the blankets and forced herself back to sleep, convincing herself that her mind was just playing tricks on her.

DRAGONS

There were many types of dragons during the reign of King Melagolin. The dragons originated from the Mythical Valley. When the dragons reached a certain age, their magic would begin to develop. Ancient old dragons had the ability to turn themselves into humans; this is when their eyes would turn a flaming green. When dragons were born, which was not too often, their eyes were either blue or purple, and they could not fly or breathe fire. Immature dragons could not fly, but they could breathe underwater and wander around the land as they matured into adult dragons. The eyes of adolescent dragons would turn silver or red, and they could start flying now. Finally, once the dragons were fully mature, their eyes would turn a flaming green. Fifty dragon years was about a hundred and fifty to two hundred human years. The Montrale monks were the first to discover the dragons. Dragons were secluded creatures and usually avoided human contact.

A REWARD

Aptos climbed down the boat and reached the shores of the Mythical Valley. Time had passed since the wedding of Nieve and King Shabah, and there had been peace in the lands but silent worry as to what Bashemdar was going to do. The poor souls that were still lingering in the seas (the Vonkerns and the Monks who were guarding the door) were just drifting on the water waiting, they grew tired and longed to return home with each passing day. Everyone else since the great decision in the Heart of the Unknown

Sea had completed their tasks returned home with their families. Bashemdar had either given up or was planning something terrible; either way, he was too much of a risk to let life, but no one had a plan as to how to get rid of him. "I have an idea, your Majesty," said Aptos. "Why not release the Sekhemet?" he said. "It is far too risky," said King Shabah. "I heard of a way to control it," said Aptos. "How?" Ask King Shabah. "There are rumors of a necklace," said the Vonkern. "Someone must know of it, and we can give that person a reward," said Aptos.

"Let us find the necklace first and see if it is true and if it is true, then we shall release the Sekhemet," said King Shabah. "I will send my servants to spread the word of the necklace. said the King. King Shabah's servants extended the message of the necklace throughout all the land of the Mythical Valley, and word spread all the way to the Kingdom of the Endless mountains and everywhere else. After the great commemoration of Nieve's wedding, the girls had returned to the Kingdom of Stone along with many of its former dwellers. Many of the old shops that had closed because of the curse had opened back up, and bakeries were filling the air once again like it had in the past. Vonkerns were beginning to visit the Kingdom once again as well. Anne and Samara were now back to being normal princesses. They were now beginning weapons training, which was a requirement for young royals and learning foreign languages.   James and Joseph just so happened to be among some of their instructors.

Also, Anne was beginning a kind of etiquette training for she was next in line to get married within a few years and so had to start learning how to be a proper Queen.   This was quite a nuisance for Anne since she was not enjoying the idea of marriage.

ALMOST RIPE

"Better Mafoo, much better..." mumbled Bashemdar to a warlock with gleaming eyes.   Bashemdar was holding a spell competition between the warlocks to see if their powers had improved.   He had plans to go and open the door where the Sekhemet was imprisoned and to do that without the key, a tremendous amount of magic was needed.   The whereabouts for the key was still unknown.   Sir Vallah had held his tongue during the interrogations.

He had been the one chosen to keep the secret of where the key hid.   Since Sir Vallah's rescue, the Knight went on a vacation (much like our soldiers when they go on leave) Sir Vallah returned to his estate and began working on his very neglected garden.   A species of swamp bunny had been eating away at his vegetables since he had left, and he began to set up traps around his plants to try and catch the annoying aquatic rodent. He planned to make a delicious pie out of it once he captured it.

ZEMALUS

Zemalus was his name. He was the conjurer with magic strong enough to turn all the dragons into mermaids, and it was only he that could change them back. His apprentices (the warlocks risen from the dead by Abigail and Bashemdar) had all turned against him because of Bashemdar.

Zemalus was the only known wizard who a fully mature dragon with flaming green eyes, had willingly given him its blood to drink.

The stronger a dragon, the stronger the person's magic became when its blood was ingested. His magical powers were remarkable after he had sipped the dragon blood, and his eyes had changed to look just like the dragon's eyes.

He even grew about an inch taller.

The Wizard Venton was one of the few under his teachings that did not turn against him. There were myths that Zemalus could even shoot fireballs from his eyes. Zemalus had vanished during the war, right after he transformed and hid the dragons in the seas of

Neros. Some thought he had transformed himself and joined them underneath the Seas of Neros.

159

A MESSAGE

The bird arrived after much flying to a family home in some cold woods. The home was isolated and housed a lovely family. The message of the necklace had been attached to its foot, and he was to take the message to anyone who may not had received word of the necklace and then return to the castle and send out another note. The bird flew to the door of the house and pecked until Ascot (the boy who found Abigail) opened the door. "It's a royal message," said the boy. "What does it say?" asked his mother. "That there will be a reward of his or her choosing within reason for whoever knows the whereabouts of a magic necklace that can control a Sekhemet," said the boy. "I didn't know that was possible said the father of Ascot" Buttinsky suddenly leaped up from underneath the table (the witch was treated much like a house cat now) and ran out the door. "Buttinsky!! Nooo!" yelled Ascot. "Come back" He cried as the goat ran off. When the witch finally arrived in the Kingdom of Stone (King Giorgio's home), she waited until a clumsy servant swung the door open and snuck in the castle. Up she went on all fours and found the King napping away on his royal bed made up of red velvet sheets and silk. The witch, making sure not to make a sound, pounced on the King waking him up" I wish to be pardoned" she said "Ahhh! said the King as he gawked at the talking goat. "Forgive me," said the goat. The goat abruptly exploded into smoke which filled the room and shifted back into the witch. "I am the keeper of the necklace that controls the Sekhemet," said the witch. "Why would you want to help me?" asked the King, still staring at the witch in disbelief.

"Bashemdar murdered my mother; the necklace was a gift she had given to me" muttered the witch. "I want him dead," growled Abigail. "There is no other way to kill Bashemdar," said the witch.

"He has the cursed blood of a dragon running through his veins. Bashemdar was the one who corrupted the pupils of Zemalus and poisoned my father and brother with evil. If you give me the key to unleash the creature, then I will give you the necklace to control it," she said....

What had occurred during the war of Melagolin before the enchanter Zemalus had disappeared after the Sekhemet had been locked away, Zemalus created a key to unlock the door and a necklace to control Zidus. Zemalus hid the key away inside a young red-headed boy (Sir Vallah) while he entrusted the necklace to Lanesta. The key could only be taken out by a spell. Zemalus also knew the Witches' mother Lanesta who was against her husband, Agarion, practicing evil magic. Lanesta had told Zemalus about Agarion's and Bashemdar's meetings where Bashemdar would teach Agarion dark secrets.

CHAPTER 5

"The servant has arrived," said King Giorgio to the soon to be pardoned, now white Witch Abigail. "Here it is your greatness" Bowed Sir Harrist as he handed the beautiful jeweled silver necklace to the King on a red velvet pillow. Sir Harrist had gone to fetch the necklace that controlled the Sekhemet from the witch's home in the human world and brought it back to King Giorgio.

"Lady Abigail," said King Giorgio.

"You have spoken the truth to me.

The key is within my finest Knight Sir Vallah. You and the great Wizard Venton may extract the key from him and unleash Zidus as you asked" Thank you, your Majesty" bowed the redeemed witch. The Wizard Venton and the witch now left on their way to Sir Vallah's home to extract the key from within him.

EXCELLENT

"Excellent!" said Bashemdar as he applauded a warlock.

Excellent, he said. The warlocks were now ready. It had taken them months to finally recover. When the warlocks had been raised from the dead, their bodies had slowly started regenerating. Their skin was slowly growing back, and their eyes were forming again as though they were alive again, but once they were complete, you could still tell that they had died. The warlocks looked much like vampires. In fact, that is what they had turned into since they had died before. Unlike true vampires, though, because they were wizards in life, they had magic. Imagine a vampire with magic like a wizard that did not need blood to survive. That is what these warlocks became like. They had pale transparent skin, but no fangs and practiced magic with cold eyes that glowed at night. Still a bit slow though, their brains still could not fully function as they used to when they were alive. They had memory problems, but it was possible to get back.

FLIES

"She is helping us get rid of Bashemdar," said Venton. "She has been forgiven by the King and is now on our side," said the wizard to the bewildered Knight. Sir Vallah was in his morning clothes cooking a delicious swamp bunny stew (the swamp bunny that had been eating his garden) while the two enchanters sat at his breakfast table sipping delicious warm red flower tea. "This is so delicious said the witch. Abigail had changed since her pardon. She seemed warm-hearted and even a little nice like a grandma that bakes cookies for kids since she had made the deal with the King to get rid of Bashemdar. Sadly, she still was not easy on the eyes, although her heart had changed. "The thing is..." said Sir Vallah as he coughed a little after sipping some tea nearly choking at her appearance. "You need a certain type of spell with certain ingredients to get the key out of me" If the key is just taken out of me, it will not work," said the Knight. "I know which spell it is," said Venton. "I was a student of the one who bestowed it on you" Splat" Abigail smashed a fly and then flicked it off the table. The poor soul was still twitching as it landed on the floor. "Well good then, how about we do this in your home," said the Knight trying to ignore what he just saw. "Good idea," said Abigail grimacing proud of the life she had just taken.

"I hate insects," said the redeemed witch.

BATTLE TRAINING

"I think the girls are ready" Smiled James as he looked Samara and Anne over, proud of their exam results" "You two shall be great warriors," said Joseph in agreement with his brother. Anne and Samara were going to take part in taking out Bashemdar as part of their training.

Future queens needed knowledge and experience in battle to rule a kingdom, whether they got married or not.

They needed to make logical decisions to aid their husbands or command knights, depending on how the couple wanted to make decisions. Anne had become great with the sword, and Samara had a talent with magic.

It had been arranged for Samara to seek further training in magic under a wizard while Anne would continue learning battle strategies on the ship that was guarding the door. After the girls basic training, whatever they seemed exceptionally talented in they would get referred for more training to make it their specialty.

HE IS BACK

The bird flew and flew. Zemalus had just finished delivering a royal message to a small boy named Ascot. Zemalus had turned himself into a bird during the battle of Melagolin. It was a secret between him and the Wizard Venton.

Zemalus had been ashamed of what had happened in the past. It hurt his heart so much that all of his disciples had turned against him. There was no more magic in the land like there used to be in the past. He also thought that if Bashemdar had not really died, he would never reveal himself if Zemalus was around. Now that Bashemdar had come back from hiding (Bashemdar was also trying to hide from Zemalus) Zemalus knew he needed to be destroyed.

THE SONS OF HENRY

The first son of Henry drank the green mixture. He felt nothing, but then he felt everything inside of him had changed.

What had happened, in the very beginning, when Henry and his sons came into the other place or portal whatever it was, he did not actually discover it on his own. Something had been watching him through all his sorrows that he experienced from the loss of his wife. It longed to have the love that his deceased wife had. It was an enchantress of some kind, she changed herself to look like his wife, and she had been a ruler in the land. When Henry and his sons went through the portal that the Enchantress had created, she lured Henry and his sons and decided to make them part of her world.

After they married the witch and Henry divided the lands and physically changed their sons with magical potions. One of the sons, the first son, became the first Montrale monk and left and created his own Kingdom. The second son developed magic abilities after drinking the potion and became the descendant of the Kingdom of Stone. The third son also developed magical abilities but stronger than the second son. He became the ancestor of all the wizards and witches unrelated to the second son. The drinking of the potion was meant to be a blessing bestowed on the boys and a welcoming to the discovered land. The fourth son developed into something unexpected.

Eric had a different reaction to the potion and became a Sekhemet.

LET ME DO IT

The warlocks were now on their way to the Kingdom of Stone and the Kingdom of the Endless Mountains. When the warlocks who were headed to the Kingdom of the Stone (what used to be the Petrified Kingdom that Abigail had cursed) they were to split, and half of them would continue to through the swamp to the World Beneath. "Let me do it," said Zemalus. He had finally arrived at the home of Venton where he and Abigail had been trying to figure out how to remove the key from Sir Vallah.

"Oh my!" Exclaimed Venton. "This should be no surprise to you," said Zemalus to Venton.

"You knew this would happen," said the wizard. "I did everything as you taught me and it's not working," said Venton. "Yes, but it needed this," said Zemalus. Zemalus unexpectedly spit into a large mixing pot, and it exploded then sizzled, making a loud whistle sound. "Now give it to him," he said. Abigail filled a cup with the mixture that Zemalus had spit into and offered it to Sir Vallah.

With a very disgusted look on his face, Sir Vallah drank the potion, and like a cat coughing up a hairball the Knight heaved out the key" I would be proud" said Abigail complimenting the knights vomiting abilities. The witch scooped up the key and fled the house of Venton.

Off she went into the sky, she had now turned herself into a fruit bat and was headed to the door beneath the waters to release the creature.

SAILOR FABLES

"My father was a great, great warrior," said Aptos.

Anne rolled her eyes as she felt her ears might begin to bleed. Anne had joined Aptos and the others that had been on the ship for some time now guarding the door where Zidus was kept. Aptos entertained Anne with the same story repeatedly. He sounded like a broken record. The ship that was guarding the door had become much like a duty station.

The way that soldiers get assigned somewhere for some time and then must leave and then new soldiers arrive. "Legolas was his name," said a proud Aptos. Anne was on the verge of tears. "Why me," she thought. "Why couldn't I have been better at magic and not have to endure this tedious adventure" she thought to herself.

"Excuse me," said Anne as she dismissed herself from Aptos's presence.

"I have to pee," she lied.

ON THEIR WAY

"Has she unleashed the creature yet?" asked King Giorgio. I don't know, but she is headed that way. "said Venton speaking about Abigail. The wizard returned to the King who was in route to the ship where Anne was on while Abigail had arrived at the waters between the Mythical Valley and the Heart of the Unknown Sea. "I shall wear the necklace as soon as I arrive; by then the creature will probably already be released," said the King.

Meanwhile, Sir Vallah returned to his home; he still did not want to take part in anything he did not have to. He felt he had experienced enough with the night bird when he had been trapped inside the cave with the hallow tree and then suffering interrogation from Bashemdar's warlocks. Zemalus though, headed towards the Seas of Neros after the witch had turned herself into a fruit bat. He had his own plans to take care of.

FIRE

"The castle is on fire! The castle is on fire!" Samara sat up. "Oh no, not this dream again," thought the Princess to herself. Samara had been experiencing the same dream again repeatedly a couple of nights a week, but this time it was not a dream; this was real.

The warlocks had found a way to arrive at the Kingdom sooner than expected and had really set the castle on fire. *"Samara," she heard. Samara saw the strange figure again that led her out into the hallway and down some stairs.*

"I'll be waking up again soon," she thought. "Samara this way," whispered the voice.

Samara decided to follow the voice this time. "I'll change the dream this time she thought" The Princess stepped outside the castle and she saw lights in the sky, it was coming from the warlocks shooting fire all around and trying to destroy the Kingdom. What had been happening to the Princess was that Penelope's soul had been watching over her and had led her out of the castle, for in that instant when Samara left her room and walked down the stairs a warlock set her room on fire, had she not followed Penelope's voice Samara would not have survived. "Come, my dear, come," said Joseph as he suddenly appeared in front of the Princess.

Joseph once again took the Princess over his shoulder and evacuated her out of the Kingdom.

RETURN OF THE DRAGONS

Zemalus began to walk along the shore then he began to say something in that strange enchanter language that sounded like a mixture of French and Arabic. He lifted his hands up and began to sprinkle something into the waters. The water began to change green, and foam began to rise to the surface. He had gone to the Seas of Neros. Zemalus was calling up the mermaids and changing them back into their true form.

"Welcome back," he said as he looked at the dragons who were standing on the beach.

I need your help. Bashemdar has returned and is back to his old tricks again.

He is destroying the Kingdom of Stone, and we are going to release the Sekhemet. Agarion's daughter has sided with us, and she has given us the necklace.

Let us go now and save the Kingdoms" Bellowed the wise old wizard. "Off they flew with Zemalus riding on one of the dragons to the Kingdom of Stone.

ZIDUS IS RELEASED

Down went the bat deep into the water, Aptos and Anne only caught a glimpse of what happened. Anne thought it was the oddest thing in the world. Imagine being out on a boat, and then a bat holding a key decides to go swimming. It is just so odd. Anyway, it was the witch. Down she went, overwhelmed with joy and she put the key into the hole somehow with her little bat foot (strange that she did not turn herself into a fish, so she could at least breathe underwater) and unlocked it. Zidus was released. Up he went, and opposite the direction of the boat that Aptos was on, the creature that all were terrified of was finally free and away it went heading in the direction of the Mythical Valley. Then lightning struck twice. Out came the witch paddling along and climbing up the side of the boat still in bat form and coughing and spitting out water. "Bahahaha," chuckled the bat. "Bashemdar will not stand a chance" laughed the bat. "Where are the King and the wizard?" said Aptos to the bat realizing it was the pardoned witch. "Oh, I left those two silly fools behind," said the bat still smiling. "I'm sorry, I was supposed to do something else?" asked the bat now looking concerned.

"You must go and tell the King and the wizard (Giorgio and the wizard were riding on camels halfway through the swamp above the World Beneath) to head to the Mythical Valley and guide the creature to the Kingdom of Stone," said Aptos. (A different bird had flown by the boat and told of how the Kingdom of Stone had caught on fire) "The rest of us will leave and go and head towards the frozen mountains and try and destroy Bashemdar's home," he said. "Oh, do be careful, said the witch, that used to be my home" Off went the bat (the Witch Abigail) towards the swamp now and Aptos with Anne and all his men began heading back to shore to start their new mission. "We shall headfirst to the World Beneath to get some camels," said Aptos" I don't feel like traveling on foot" Grumbled the aged Vonkern.

BIRD DROPPINGS

"I'm tired," said the King. "Let's take a break shall we, the kingdoms are at stake, but if the leaders aren't well-rested what good is it to save them," said the wizard. Giorgio and the wizard stopped their camels and sat on a large stone in the middle of the swamp. "Here, have some," said the King as he handed the wizard some tea. "Mmmm....smells delicious" "I wonder said the King. Then without warning, bird poop landed on his head.

It was the witch; she had now turned herself into a bird. "We must head to the Kingdom of stone," said the witch "Chirp! Chirp!" she said.

King Giorgio wiped his face angrily then he picked up a rocked and popped that witch on the side. "ARRRRGGG! cried the witch in pain. "The Kingdom is on fire, and Aptos and your daughter are heading towards the frozen Mountains. "Very well... thank you," said the wizard. "Go and tell Sir Harrist Madam that we need a lift" "Indeed" Squawked Abigail who now flew off to find Sir Harrist. "Old Hag.' mumbled King Giorgio to himself as he saw Abigail fly off. Moments later, Sir Harrist appeared (he happened to be close by; he had been looking for the King). "Great to see you, my friend," said Venton.

Up they climbed including Abigail onto the dragon's back and off they went leaving behind the camels and headed towards the Mythical Valley.

THE ULTIMATE BATTLE

Finally, the warlocks and Bashemdar had arrived at the Kingdom of the Endless Mountains. They began to do what the other warlocks did to the Kingdom of Stone and set it on fire.

The citizens of that Kingdom began to run out and scream in all directions. Many of the warlocks were harassing the women of the land.

Unexpectedly, Zemalus appeared out of nowhere on top of a dragon headed straight toward Bashemdar. "This must stop!" said Zemalus. "You can't hurt me," said Bashemdar to Zemalus. "I have the blood of a dragon within me just as you" Snickered the dark warlock. Zemalus jumped off the dragon, and the two warlocks began casting fire spells at each other and took turns shocking each other! It was a great sight to see. The battle went on and finally, King Giorgio, and the Sekhemet arrived. King Giorgio tossed the necklace to Venton, who now ordered the Zidus to eat the dark warlock. The war was over, and now the Sekhemet was directed to go back to the door beneath the waters. Aptos and his men moved onto the warlocks who attacked the other places and killed most of them. The few that survived vanished to unknown places; after months had passed, the Kingdoms were being rebuilt. Zemalus was welcomed back into the Kingdom of Stone like old times, and he opened his own academy of magic once again without fear of Bashemdar corrupting his students. Samara joined the academy along with Nieve and Anne who all became Queens and enjoyed riding camels in the desert in the land of the World Beneath with James and Joseph on their vacations.

King Giorgio grew old and grey and happy. He became surrounded with at least thirty grandchildren and enjoyed telling them tales of when he was young by a warm fire each night. The dragons that were once mermaids all returned to the Land of the Mythical Valley, and Sir Vallah no longer took part in battles, he put in for early retirement and occasionally visited Petry and the Wizards Venton and Zemalus. And finally, Abigail decided to go back to the human world after Zemalus put a beautifying spell on her and remarried another man.

This time a bookkeeper...

The Pirates of the Unknown Sea

Book 3

CHAPTER 1

The apparition went back into the sea; the crew had just overcome the most heartbreaking event in their lives. Into the fog it went, its glowing eyes watching them with deep emotion as the waters consumed it, silently hoping that someday it would return. Their hearts began to tear; the thing was not always so; it still vaguely resembled what it had been in life. It could not help what it had become, it was a result from what happened, the catastrophe, and the crew began to mourn. "It's my fault" wept the Captain as he bowed his head in sadness and tears streamed down his face. "It was inevitable, Captain, don't be so hard on yourself," said Morven. "Besides," he said, "there's still hope."

THE CATASTROPHE

Time had passed since the reigns of the three Queens whose kingdoms were now gone. The kingdoms and the World Beneath had changed dramatically. Everyone had moved on with their lives after the final battle and forgotten something extremely important. Everyone forgot about Zidus. The necklace used to control him was lost, and the key to the door holding him back was misplaced. The Sekhemet had grown bitter once again for being abandoned beneath the waters, overtime his resentment grew into hate, and the creature returned full of vengeance. When the monster arose to the surface, it brought with it catastrophe.

Zidus drowned out all the land killing most of the population and blocked out all the light with a thick continuous fog; then he silently demanded that certain souls in the land would die prematurely and go beneath the waters in an endless purgatory wandering the Unknown Seas.

The souls beneath the waters could be seen from above. They grew tired from wandering, and as though experiencing a second death would slowly decay again. Zidus wanted them to feel what he felt from being locked away for so long. Misery. The beautiful forests that had existed were now dying, and it was as though the entire world had ended, and everything was grey. Only small islands existed now since most of the land had been destroyed and there was still some vegetation, but not much and everyone had to change their way of life.

Most had become pirates or scavengers who would just sail around seeking food or the necklace which over time seemed more like a myth. Only two seasons were left in the world, cold and frozen. Oddly, mostly everyone liked when the season was frozen since the people could stop sailing around and walk on the frozen waters as though it was land. When people looked down into the waters, the poor souls entrapped by Zidus appeared like glimmering blind creatures. At times, the ghosts were so brain fogged (if they still had a brain it was frozen) they would slam into things like sharks' mouths or big rocks and so on.

THE LONE PIRATE

He sighed. His meal was almost done. He had been cooking a fish over a fire and could not wait to eat. It was Xalder, the lone pirate with silver eyes. This man lived alone most of his life; he was the last Montrale Monk from a place called the Mythical Valley from the World Before. For years he sailed alone in his tiny ship and explored the Unknown Seas. As he continued cooking his fish, someone had been stalking him. Whiskers. Whiskers was a feral woman with a beard that looked like cat whiskers. There were not very many women left in this frozen land and much like the lone pirate, she also traveled alone but close to Xalder. Whiskers would keep her distance, but when Xalder had his guard down (usually when he was asleep), she would steal things from him, usually food. She seemed to be appearing more often than usual lately. It had been about a year since Xalder rescued her, she had been caught up in some sort of trap set up by other pirates who were hoping to capture a deer, but instead they captured Whiskers. Xalder set her free, and when she was freed, she ran as fast as she could and hid. She looked like a golden gorilla but shorter and slimmer. After that incident, she began to follow Xalder like a lost puppy and go wherever he would go but never got too close. Xalder enjoyed her brief company when she would appear even though she could not speak. She was slowly beginning to understand small words like food or water, but she still could not pronounce the words. Her attempts at speaking sounded like animal sounds. He had made up his mind that one of these days he was going to shave her.

He wanted to see what she looked like beneath all her golden fur. Mabey, he would give her a Mohawk.

BAD DREAMS

"This was it" thought the Captain. He had had enough, and he could not bear the loss of his son any longer. He just wanted the pain to end. He arrived on the edge of a cliff and took his last deep breath looking down around at the beautiful woods around him. "I never got to explore these beautiful woods" he thought, then suddenly he changed his mind. "I want to live," he thought. The Captain glanced down at the rocks below then turned around, and as he turned around, he slipped on some loose gravel and fell to the rocks below. "Ahhh," he screamed. *Splat*. The Captain woke up. "That's just wrong," thought the Captain. "Even my dreams are wrong," he mumbled. "Captain" whispered a voice from the darkness. "Captain," it said again. It was Morven. "Are you all right? Are you having those blasted dreams again?" He asked. Morven had been a wanderer before until the Captain, and his crew had come upon him. After being invited to join the crew, Morven swore to always be loyal to the Captain and do whatever the Captain asked. One time during the frozen season a member of the crew lied to Morven, telling him that the Captain asked him to lick a pole and he did. Morven's tongue froze to the pole, and he was stuck there all night while the other members of the crew had gone off-board and sat by a fire and drank tasty mint ale while Morven froze all night with his tongue to the pole.

Morven got his revenge eventually though; he found a type of poison ivy plant and put some of its leaves in the other crew members' bedding. The next day the other crew members were itching and had red boils on their skin. To cure their suffering, Morven had them bathe in animal feces, which worked. After that, no one tried to prank Morven again. "It's this blasted anxiety; it's overwhelming, and I just don't feel like myself," said the Captain. "Why don't we go for a walk and see if that doesn't help. Here, have some of my red flower tea," said Morven as he handed the Captain a warm cup of sweet red flower tea. It was extremely delicious. "Thank you," said the Captain with a smirk. "You are such a good pirate," he said. "I know" admitted Morven proudly with a smile. "It's because I owe you my life, Captain."

MYSTERIOUS CAVE

"Oh...Oh.... Ahhh... ahhhh..." Xalder heard as he awoke from his sleep. "Oh," he heard again. It was Whiskers. She was grunting and jumping up and down and pointing at something while staring at Xalder.

"Oh.... Oh... grunted the bearded woman. Xalder sat up and began to follow Whiskers. After what seemed like hours, she led him to a hidden cave in the ground, which strangely had a lit torch at the entrance, and beckoned him to follow her. As they walked through the cave, they arrived at a large opening which had paintings depicting what looked like an event, and Xalder noticed the painting of a key and a necklace. "Interesting," he thought. "Oh," said Whiskers, who now gripped Xalder by the hand and pulled him through a different tunnel leading him out of the open room. "I'm coming, I'm coming," he said to her. The two continued carefully walking through the narrow tunnel, and then light began to appear at the end. Xalder realized the light was coming from below, he put out the torch, and they arrived at the edge of a cliff. Xalder peered down and saw the most unimaginable thing...more bearded women. There were at least twenty bearded women, and they seemed to be performing a strange ritual. All of them were danc-ing around a large fire, and they were speaking! "The chosen one has come! The chosen one has come!" They chanted. Unexpected-ly, Whiskers let out a loud yelp and then she pushed Xalder to the fire below.

OLD MYTHS

"My father told me that you must die to get the key," Said the Cap-tain. "That doesn't make sense," said Morven. "Supposedly the key is somewhere beneath the waters" continued Captain Ron. The two had been chatting away until early morning and were now heading back to the ship.

Lorraine was the ship's name. The Captain had named her after his one true love.

Lorraine was a brunette woman with a beard. When the Captain had decided that he wanted to go searching for the key and the necklace, Lorraine stayed behind on a small island in a hut that she and the Captain had been living out of. He remembered running his fingers through her dark soft bunny like fur when she would fall asleep. He missed her so badly and wondered what she might be doing in that moment. He missed how warm she kept him at night. He did not even need a blanket.

OUCH

Xalder blinked, his face hurt, and he began to look around. He was lying on his back on the cold hard ground by smoldering fire embers, and he could smell delicious food. "Welcome," said Whiskers. "So, you do speak," he said. "Yes," said Whiskers, then she grabbed the top of her hair and pulled. She had been wearing a mask. "Why?" asked Xalder. Whiskers then began to explain the origin of the bearded women. What had happened long ago when the catastrophe had hit, and the climate changed, a group of women with excellent hunting skills had discovered this gigantic cave with tunnels and decided to stay and make it a home. The women captured as many black furry camels as they could before they would go extinct and bred them. When the camels would die, the women would use their fur as clothes to keep warm and to disguise themselves. The disguise kept them safe from pirates since they were usually mistaken as animals.

"That's smart," said Xalder. "Why did you finally decide to bring me here?" he asked. "Because you're the chosen one," she said.

MONSTER DREAMS

The young man had noticed that his father had changed since his mother's passing. Henry, the boy's father, had become reserved and was neglecting his normal duties.

He seemed obsessed over something, but he would not say what it was. One evening when his father had secluded himself in his bedroom, Eric went over and knocked on the door. Suddenly, the door flung open, and a monster appeared! "Raaaaar!" Growled the hideous beast. Zidus awoke. He had been dreaming about the time before he had ingested his stepmother's potion, which turned him into the creature he was now.

A MAP

Long, long ago, before the world had been hit with the catastrophe, there was an old enchanter who had hidden the key of his book of spells away in separate places. He had foreseen what was going to come and so decided he would try to leave future generations hope. There was absolutely nothing he could do to prevent the future arising of Zidus, but he could leave behind his book of spells and the key to lock up Zidus once again if it ever became possible.

TIME TO SAIL

"Back to Lorraine," said the Captain." I am done with my mourning, and it is time to resume our mission," he said, as the crew began to set up sail on Lorraine. What had happened, in the beginning of the story, the Captain with his crew and his son (from Lorraine) had volunteered to go and look for the map that the last great wizard,

Venton had left behind. The Captain and his crew, except for Morven, were from an island in the east part of the world rumored to have been the Heart of the Unknown Sea. That land is where creatures known as Vonkerns, who some say were aliens, co-existed with Montrale Monks. This Island, now called Crescent, because of its shape, was where most of the pirates were from. When Zidus flooded the World Beneath, the Heart of the Unknown Sea (Which had been a bigger island) had risen and broken through the World Beneath over the Seas of Neros. The Seas of Neros and the waters from Zidus had become one vast ocean covering all the land. The land above the World Beneath (The Swamp and the Kingdom of Stone), and the World Beneath (what used to be the home of the Vonkerns) were all underwater now. It was a small village where people lived mostly out of huts, and they taught their children how to hunt and fish.

The villagers usually occupied themselves with making or repairing ships, and they had divided themselves into groups that had agreed to rotate off the island in search of the legendary map left behind by Venton. It was only during the cold season, not the frozen season when the pirates would leave Crescent. While one crew was out searching for the map, another was out exploring and gathering supplies or bringing back new citizens. That was how the Captain's wife (Lorraine) had been found and brought back.

So anyway, while the Captain and his crew were out, the curse of Zidus had struck and taken his son prematurely. The lightning had only half killed Romus (the Captain's son), his soul was sucked out of his body and pulled into the waters where he was now wandering the seas with the other countless souls wandering around. Zidus usually claimed a life with lightning, and there was no telling who or when he would take a life. It was believed that if someone killed Zidus, the waters would cease, and the world would go back to what it once was, and the souls he had claimed would come back to life or die completely and finally be free.

CHAPTER 2

"Yo ho... ho... yo... he... he..., I love this wandering life for me!" Sang a pirate. "I can't imagine a different world from the one we are in," he said as he glanced at his brother. "Me neither," said another. There they went, three young men, sailing along in some vast unexplored place where the Endless Mountains had once existed. "So, who was this great Sir Vallah," asked one of them. "He was a knight in shining armor; he was the one chosen to keep the key." "Well, obviously the old boy didn't do a good job at keeping the key because look how the world is today" "That be true, that be true" agreed his brother. "Say, where do you think our littlest brother went off too?" "I don't know, but let's keep sailing and looking."

PAINTINGS

"After we eat, I'll take you back to the open room and tell you about the painting," said Whiskers. The woman had decided to keep the name Whiskers since she had grown used to it and found it amusing. "Thank you," she said as she glanced up at Xalder with a smile. "For what?" he asked. "For the name, I like it," she said while eating some stew. "This is delicious," said Xalder. "What is it?" he asked, "It's an ancient recipe called swamp bunny stew." "It hits the spot." "Yes, it does," he agreed. When the two finally finished eating, Whiskers took the lone pirate with silver eyes back to the open room where she had pushed him down.

She took him to a spot where there were paintings that had been made from the women's ancestors. "It depicts the world before the catastrophe," she said.

"How long do you think it's been?" he asked. "How long has what been?" asked Whiskers. "The catastrophe." "Oh, according to great Mama, it's about a hundred years" "I'll take you to her, and she can explain everything to you." Said Whiskers. "Great Mama was a little girl when she saw it happen," said Whiskers. "We think she is the last of her kind. She is the great, great, great-granddaughter of the White Witch Abigail who had defeated Zidus before" said Whiskers.

FROZEN IS COMING

It was almost that time again, when Zidus would rise and freeze the waters. All were beginning to return home as they did every time the cold season would end and watch as the waters would freeze over. This was the time when the fog would really thicken, and most of the pirates had gone back to Crescent. Those that were left out would suffer more than those that had returned. If a ship was out at sea when Zidus froze the waters, the pirates would have to return home on foot or wait until the cold weather came before they could sail back, but this was not good since the ship would usually end up severely damaged from the ice. A wintry wind would begin to blow, and new snow would begin to fall, and the strange bird would begin to appear once again. There was a strange bird that would come out of hiding only during the frozen season. It was said that the bird was a giant and that it had also been part of the curse from Zidus. It had a wingspan of about thirty feet, and when it screeched, it shook the ground and could be heard for miles. The bird would hunt down people, but no one ever claimed to see it eating human. The bird looked like a giant black eagle with flaming blue eyes, quite beautiful. Since the curse of Zidus, this bird was seen flying around the first few days of the frozen season and only seen on occasion the rest of the time.

SIGHTINGS

"Shurn, Clark and Brag are their names Captain" said Morven who had been talking about his brothers.

What had happened when Captain Ron had found Morven wandering around before he was part of the crew, Morven had been separated from his brothers. They were like our urban explorers. They never enjoyed settling down anywhere and would just sail around on their own in the ship they had built as kids with their father. During one of their explorations, Clark had seen something glowing in the distance, he had separated from the others and began following something that looked like a wisp. The wisp led him to something that looked like a necklace petrified in a rock. When Clark returned to his brothers and tried to lead them to the necklace, he could not find his way back to it and so they just decided to go back to their ship and sail on. Morven remembered that Clark had seen this necklace somewhere southwest where the Endless Mountains were said to have been, which is where his brothers were last seen sailing around by Morven when he got lost. "We shall head in that direction then," said the Captain. "The legend says that the necklace controls the creature." And so, off they went.

GREAT MAMA

"You may call me Ivene." Said Great Mama as she studied Xalder's face lifting his chin with her hand. "Yes," she said. "I believe he can do it. He truly is a Montrale Monk," said Great Mama." "You must get the ingredients so that I can do the transformation and you two can go beneath the waters and get the key. Great Mama knew where the key to lock up Zidus was found. It was below the Unknown Seas and the only way to get it was by being transformed by a spell which would allow someone to breathe underwater. Great Mama was the last human born with magic blood left in the world, and so she sent Whiskers and Xalder back to his camp, which would take a few days travel to prepare for their long journey to get the key. Ivene needed an egg from the giant bird that came out during the frozen season to complete the potion to transform Xalder and Whiskers.

STUCK IN ICE

"We must hurry" grumbled Shurn as his slow; moving brothers were trying to set sail. "It's getting closer to frozen time, and I don't want to be stuck out here in who knows what with you two dingbats!" The three brothers had decided to take a break by a small island that they noticed as they were sailing along trying to get back to a camp they had set up before they had lost their brother Morven. They had stocked up on some food and made a kind of shelter by the camp. There was not much food left on the ship, and Shurn wanted to at least get the ship on a beach so that it would not be damaged by the ice. "What is that," said Brag as he now listened like a meerkat perched upon his legs pointing towards the sky. "I think I saw him," he said with much concern. "What," said Clark. "It's not time yet," he said. "He doesn't come out until frozen has come; the waters are still water," he said. The ship began to vibrate, and the giant bird with the flaming blue eyes came out of the fog and began to head towards them. "What do we do!

What do we do!" Exclaimed Clark. "Ahhhh" screamed Brag as the bird suddenly, with the speed of lightning swooped down and lifted Shurn by the arms and flew

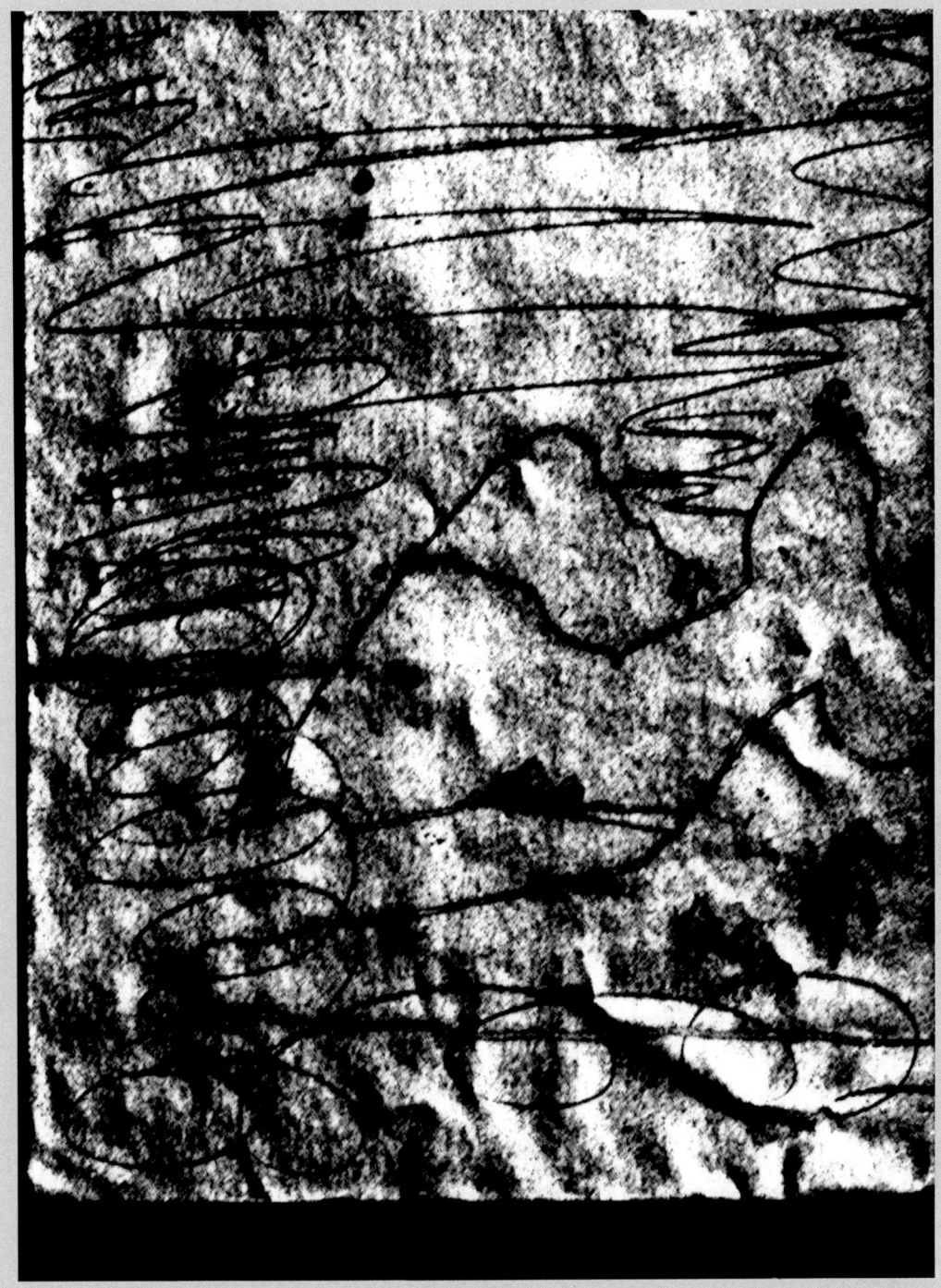

away. "Nooo!" whispered Brag. "No, no..no!" he cried in agony as he saw his dear brother carried away by a monstrous beast.

CHAPTER 3

It had finally come. The land was now frozen and whatever ships had been out at sea were either damaged by the ice and its passengers had to now race back home on foot before the cold season came or stay by their ships or find an island and try to survive. Whiskers and Xalder finally arrived back at his camp where his ship was and began to prepare for their journey. "I think I've seen its nest before," said Xalder. "Here, this is for you," said Whiskers as she tossed him a bag. Xalder opened the bag and pulled out a set of furry pants and a top like the one Whiskers was wearing. "Nice," he said, and he began to put them on. "They fit and wow," he gasped. "They are quite warm," he said. "Let's camp here tonight, and tomorrow we shall head out." Xalder then lit a small fire, and the two talked about Great Mama and Whiskers shared with him the knowledge that she had obtained from Ivene about the world before the catastrophe.

CAPTAIN RON

Years back, one of the times when it was Captain Ron's turn to rotate out to sea to get supplies for the Pirates on Crescent, when the eternal fog seemed thicker than normal something strange had been going on near Lorraine. It was as though something large was stalking the crew and swimming beneath them. When the Captain went to investigate and peered down cautiously by the edge of Lorraine, he saw two large devilish eyes gawking out at him from the dark, murky waters. Ron took a large spear just in time. The creature suddenly tried to climb onto Lorraine. It was a huge greenish slimy octopus with ten tentacles and claws at the end. The Captain had sliced off one of its arms and sent it whimpering back into the Sea. He later turned the skin from that arm into a belt and wore it daily. He named that creature Molly. When the frozen season was approaching, and he and his crew were almost to Crescent, he thought he saw Molly following close behind. He could sense that Molly was angry, and she wanted her arm back. Nothing ever happened, but every now and then, Captain Ron thought he could see Molly following him, waiting for him, wanting revenge.

THE LEGEND OF THE CHOSEN ONE

Before the catastrophe, when the Wizard Venton had foreseen the downfall of the World Beneath, he also saw in his visions, the chosen one. The chosen one would be the last of his kind from a place called the Mythical Valley. The Mythical Valley had been the place where dragons and Montrale Monks were from. There were no more dragons in the world, and no one knew that the lone pirate was the last of his kind. It had to be the Montrale Monk to save them. Venton, inside his book of spells which he later gave to Abigale (the great, great, great, grandmother of Ivene), recorded the story of the chosen one and how he would be the one to find the key. The tribe of the bearded women had been taking care of Great Mama for a hundred years and were always on the lookout for the chosen one. No one knew the exact time when he would arrive, but they knew he would be a loner with silver eyes and so the story of the chosen one had been passed on from generation to generation.

AVENGE OUR BROTHER

"We shall avenge our brother!" said Clark after mourning the loss of Shurn. "Agreed," said Brag. The two had spent quite some time on the boat depressed and sobbing and were now exhausted, and they were heading in the direction where they saw the bird carry off Shurn. "He was the wisest one among us." said Clark. "yes, he was" agreed Brag. As the two kept walking on, a wisp suddenly appeared. It was the same wisp that Clark had seen before when they had sailed in the area where the Endless Mountains used to exist. "It's a wisp," said Clark. "That's the thing I followed that led me to the strange rock," he said. The wisp suddenly landed on top of Clark's head, and when he tried to grab it, it quickly got away and began to lead him away. "We need to look for the bird," said Brag. "Hold on," said Clark as he continued following the wisp over a hill. "Look...look...down there," he pointed "See, this thing is trying to show us something" There they were, Whiskers and Xalder. They were sitting over a fire and sipping something.

It was a good thing that they had taken their masks off, or else they would have been mistaken for animals. "Hey!" yelled Clark. "Heeey," he said. "Oh, hi," said Xalder. "We come in peace," said Clark. " "I'm Clark, and this is Brag. Have you happened to see a giant blackbird?" he asked. Whiskers glanced at Xalder now rubbing her chin. " You can't miss it," said Clark. "No," said Whiskers. "Have you seen a giant black bird," asked Whiskers. "Yes," said Clark " It carried off our brother, and we're trying to hunt it down" When they finally figured out, they were looking for the same bird. They decided to look for it together, but first, it was time to eat.

FEATHERS

The bird screeched in pain. Shurn had gotten a hold of its head feathers and managed to climb on top of its back. "You're going to do what I said bird!" growled Shurn. The bird was now trying to flip around and get Shurn off it's back. Shurn ripped another feather out from the bird's head, and the bird screeched in agony. "Each time you don't listen, you're going to lose a feather, pretty soon you're going to be bald," said the angry pirate. This continued for a while until the bird finally noticed a pattern. Each time it tried to flip Shurn over, a feather was ripped out. When the bird flew straight and steady, Shurn patted it nicely on the head. Finally, the bird was trained just like a horse, and when Shurn tugged it right, the bird now knew to turn right. Now, he needed to figure out how to get the bird to land.

Shurn grabbed the bird's head and faced it towards the ground. The bird hesitated, but it didn't want to lose another feather, so it headed down and landed headfirst into the snow. Shurn fumbled off and then sat up. "Good bird," he said. Suddenly, the bird now realizing that Shurn was off its back began to chase and peck at Shurn.

DAMAGED

"She's damaged," said the Captain. "My Beloved Lorraine" Lorraine was frozen in the ice, and the crew were continuing their search for the map on foot. "I think I saw something" exclaimed Morven. "What," said the Captain. Instantly, they were surrounded. "Run," he yelled, but it was too late. A group of bearded women ambushed the crew, tied them up, and marched them to their cave.

"Welcome," said Great Mama as she walked into the open room (the room with cave paintings) greeting the pirates.

I am the last of my kind." she said.

"I understand you are seeking the map, well, I have sent out the Chosen One with my trustee to get the egg from the giant black bird so that I may complete a breathing spell on them" "How did you know we were seeking the map," asked Captain Ron. "My girls were following you, and they overheard," she replied. "Oh," said the Captain. "What's the breathing-spell and who is the Chosen One?" Asked the Pirate.

Great Mama explained everything to them while serving them some hot stew.

THE NEST

"There it is," said Brag, the four had finally found the nest. As Whiskers and Xalder began to pick up one of the eggs (it was about 5 feet high and weighed about 180 pounds) Clark and Brag began to call out for Shurn. "I don't think it ate him," said Brag. "I don't see any human flesh or bones anywhere." The four decided that they would return to the cave with the bearded women except for Brag. He wanted to stay behind and see if Shurn would show up. "I'll come back after this," said Clark as he baded his brother farewell. Meanwhile, since Shurn had fallen off the bird, and it had chased him and tried to peck at him all this time, Shurn somehow managed once again to climb on top of its back and had been flying around trying to find the camp that he and his brothers were trying to get to before the frozen season came.

Shurn found his camp and landed, and he tied up the bird to a tree and was about to set it ablaze until suddenly he heard a voice. "Nooo," it said. "Nooo! Don't kill me," Shurn turned around and behind him was a wisp. "Shurn was shocked. The wisp glowed brightly behind Shurn, causing him to fall to his knees then the wisp flew into the bird's mouth, and the giant bird suddenly burst into blue fire which then sizzled away into smoke. When Shurn looked up, there stood before him a tall man with a long white beard past his neck who looked to be a thousand years old wearing a long-hooded cloak. "I am Venton," he said.

STALKED

"Mm... mm..., it looks delicious," said the creature as drool came down his snout. "It will go well with the bird eggs" it uttered in its deep nasty voice. "I agree," said its hungry companion. "Let's go back and gather the others, it looks feisty and were going to need more to be able to carry the eggs." The two creatures then turned around opposite the bird nest where they had been spying on Brag.

They traveled a few miles then disappeared into a hole in some ice and vanished. Meantime, Brag was getting frustrated since the bird, nor his brother had returned to the nest. Brag's stomach began to grumble. He was now beginning to wonder how long it would take to cook such a huge egg.

FISH LEGS

"You got it!" Exclaimed Great Mama as she glanced at the egg that Xalder, Whiskers, and Clark had fetched. "And who is this...charming freebooter" she cackled as she now fixed her eyes on Clark. "I am Clark... Clark fish legs," he said proudly. When Clark was a child, he loved to jump off the edge of his father's ship and swim for hours. He had been the first among his brothers to start to swim, and he picked it up so naturally that his father called him fish legs. "Very nice," said Great Mama, amused. It is time to prepare the spell she said. Xalder and Whiskers were taken into a room with hot springs where they had to saturate themselves for a few hours while Ivene prepared the spell with the egg. Clark decided to take a nap before returning to the nest and made friends with a few of the bearded women who found him quite attractive and begged him to tell them stories about all the places he and his brothers had explored throughout the dimming world.

COMFORTING OF THE SOULS

Back on Crescent, an old tradition was taking place; it was called the comforting of the souls.

Each year during the frozen season, since the beginning of the curse of Zidus when the first moon was beginning to rise, (There were two moons in the World Beneath after the curse of Zidus, prior to the curse there were four that would change with the four seasons that used to exist) the pirates of Crescent would wait until the moon of frozen season was directly above them and turn blue , they would create several bonfires throughout the island which could be seen even through the thick fog and eat and drink various teas and sing beautiful hymns for their loved ones who had passed away for at least eight days. It was a wonderful time of the year since everyone enjoyed the food and dances and wonderful story-telling. During this time, figures of the apparitions that had been taken prematurely by Zidus would appear in the green fires where their families could watch them drifting through the waters (they were green because of the unique type of herb that was burned in the fire that was found in the World). The souls could hear the singing, and the pirates believed that doing this was a sort of comfort to the spirits. Once the custom was completed, the moon would turn grey again, and the fires would go out, and the apparitions could no longer be seen. This would only work during that time when the frozen moon was blue and directly above.

PIRATE TRAINING

After the Comforting of the Souls had finished, it was now time for another tradition to take place. When the young boys of Crescent reached the age of thirteen, every year for the next three years the young boys had to journey with the rest of the boys from Crescent who were between the ages of twelve and sixteen to the west to the Frozen Islands on foot. The Frozen Islands were the remains of an ancient, vast mountain chain called the Frozen Mountains before the catastrophe of Zidus.

Abigale, the ancient dead witch, was said to have grown up there. Once there, the boys had to set up a type of camp and hunt their own food and build a ship.

Once the ship was completed, it would then be taken to the shores, and when the cold season came, the boys would sail back to Crescent. Each boy always had to be with a friend while there. They were not allowed to go anywhere alone for there were wolves among that land.

The oldest boy would be held responsible for anything that would happen while they were away. He had to make sure they were all safe and following rules. Each evening after dinner right before storytelling, they had to do a group count to make sure no one was missing. The oldest boy's father had to make sure he taught his sons how to lead. Once the boy completed the three years training, he would be assigned to a crew and then go through initiation. Once the initiation was completed, he would receive a tattoo that matched the rest of the crew's tattoo, and he would now be considered a real pirate. Each crew had their own unique initiation process, it usually consisted of something humiliating, and the new crew member had to keep a good attitude no matter what he had to face. If he did not, he had to go to the Frozen Islands once again and be shamed; he would end up being the oldest boy there having to take orders from the youngest boy. No one wanted to suffer that; most boys never did go through that.

OTHER PIRATES

In the northeast part of the drying grey world, there was another island which no one had discovered yet. It had been isolated the entire time. When the catastrophe had hit, some underwater volcanoes miles in front of the island had formed some remarkably high mountains blocking the view of the island.

Anyone passing by, thought they were just passing a large mountain chain sticking out from the waters.

These mountains were still fresh and forming so they were covered in black ash, and smoke and no life had come to exist on them yet. The smoke from the mountains concealed the island (which used to be the Mythical Valley and the outer most part of the Mythical Valley had crumbled and sunk while the center of it rose a bit).

Only a few of the natives from before the curse of Zidus had survived, and because of the isolation they had also evolved. The survivors who were once Montrale Monks changed. Their eyes changed to a light purple, and their hair became white. They were always beginning to grow hair all over their bodies, which looked like the hair on a newborn baby, since the climate had changed. The Montrale Monks were no strangers to the sea, for on their island, before the catastrophe, there had been an enormous lake with an island in the center of it.

It was basically an island within the island. The mythical valley had been about the size of Africa in our world, and now it was only about half that size. The Montrale Monks had built their own ships and sailed to and from the island within the island. They rarely left their island, since there was really no need to. They continued to live life as before without any major interruption from outside the high mountains. Their new leader was Master Klink.

The old traditions that Aptos (The old dead ruler of the Montrale Monks) had made were still being passed on.

WHY A BIRD?

"I have much to show you," said Venton. What had occurred prior to the great disaster, the wise sorcerer had drunk an extended life potion which added a hundred and thirty years to his life from the time of the curse. It needed him to change himself into a giant bird. Although he was not truly a bird, the spell forced him to really be like a bird, and he had to lay eggs. It was a horrific event for him and quite painful. "Why a bird" asked Shurn. "Why not just be yourself "he questioned. "I had to be some other creature for the spell to work," replied the now beet faced Magus. "Birds can fly, and that's useful when escaping a predator and the feathers kept me warm in this new climate." "I suppose," said Shurn after giving him a disapproving look. "Why didn't you share the potions with everyone else," asked the pirate, "There was only one, and it was a gift to me from a friend." "Oh," said Shurn. "Why didn't you just change sooner?" "I wanted to; I was actually trying to lure your other brother, but then when I couldn't I decided to just get you instead" "So why then, did you abduct me?" "Because it is time, I need to show you many things, and I may pass something on to you,

but I must show you everything first, so you have a clear picture"
"Ok" mumbled Shurn.

PLEASANT DREAMS

It was a beautiful sunny day, and Brag was out walking peacefully among the vast sea of lilies surrounding his dreamlike cottage. He began to pick wonderful blueberries for a pie he was going to bake later. That afternoon, in the town center, there was going to be a baking competition. Brag was dreaming. While he was at the nest still waiting for his brother and the bird, he had fallen asleep, and now the creatures that had stalked him earlier had now returned with others. "It's asleep," said the first creature. "Let's bind its feet and carry him," said the other creature. Brag was the third oldest among his brothers. Shurn was born first, then Clark, Brag and lastly Morven. Their parents had passed away long ago. They were from Crescent, but Brag's father did not agree with some of the rules of the Island, so Brags father decided to flee Crescent one cold season after he had had an intense argument with Captain Ron. Since then on, the family of six sailed away and just enjoyed life on their own.

Unfortunately, one frozen season when they had decided to make camp at a random island, lightning struck his parents. They had been chosen by Zidus and had joined the wandering souls beneath the seas. The brothers would often go at the location where the lightning had struck during the frozen season, and they could see their parents' souls wandering through the waters from the frozen clear ice above. Even in death, the souls had stayed together. The wandering souls usually drifted around close to the location of their death.

The creatures had now tied Brag's wrists and ankles and placed him on top of a large blanket and covered his nose with a cloth that had sleeping herbs in it. After he inhaled the herbs, the herbs would keep him from waking and forbade him from having nightmares and subdue his need for food. Six other creatures, which were known as Snow Terrors, now carried the eggs back to their dwelling. Snow Terrors were intelligent creatures that walked mostly on two legs measuring no more than four feet in height. They were a dark reddish-brown color with a white stripe down their spine with large black bat-like ears and four fingers with razor-sharp talons. They had wolf-like eyes and whiskers like a cat extending from their snouts and a language of their own. They could speak like a human and make sounds like a monkey but with a deeper voice. Their bodies were also covered in fur except their feet and hands, and they had tails like a fox. They were clever creatures and usually hibernated during the cold season. Not too many people had encounters with these creatures; it was exceedingly rare. Usually, there were only sightings here and there and stories that were told, but the creatures usually avoided any human contact unless they were attacked or starving. In this case, it seemed they were starving.

THE TRANSFORMATION

"It is time," said Great Mama. "Here," she said as she handed the lone pirate and Whiskers a warm beverage. "You two make a great couple. The potion will give you the ability to breathe underwater, I believe the key is somewhere inside the home of the creature where he sleeps" Augh" said Xalder "It tastes disgusting" "I'm sorry" said Ivene "I tried to make it taste the best that I could" "You need to drink it all". After Whiskers and Xalder forced themselves to drink the disgusting potion, they felt a tingling sensation around their bodies. "Do you feel anything," asked Ivene, "Yes," said Whiskers. "Come, quickly," said Great Mama. Ivene grabbed their hands and led them to the deepest part of the cave through a narrow tunnel which then led them to a pool.

"This is where you will enter into the Unknown Seas, when you go beneath, pick up some armor from the dead knights that you will see right away. The spell should be able to help you swim faster too, and it will only last about ten days at the most. You must find the key and come back within that time; otherwise, you will drown." "Here, take this," said Ivene as she handed whiskers a small jar with more of the potion. "Don't drink it now; if you need more time drink it a day before the ten days are over; if you split it in half it should give each of you seven more days." "Got it" said Whiskers. The two now felt a sharp pain on their necks and screamed in agony. "Ahhhh" cried Xalder, they fell to their knees, the sides of their necks were beginning to split. "It's gills," said Great Mama, "The pain will soon go," she said as she now began pushing them into the water. "Hurry, your sea creatures now, get into the water before you die!" she said. Xalder and Whiskers then jumped into the pool and began to swim. Their fingers had become webbed and their legs fused together with their feet becoming fins. They had been changed into mermaids.

WORRIED

She was almost to the cave of the bearded women. It was Lorraine, Captain Ron's wife. Before the comforting of the souls, she had grown worried since he had not yet returned to Crescent and decided she would go to her old home to see if by chance Great Mama or her bearded sisters had happened to see him. She had not visited them in so long. "I hope the giant bird hasn't taken him," she thought. As she traveled, she thought she heard something behind her, she paused a few times looking behind her, but each time she turned around, there was nothing. Lorraine continued... until finally she came to the Captain's ship. "Oh no," she thought. Lorraine approached the Captain's frozen ship and decided she would climb aboard it and began looking around calling the Captain, but there was no one. Exhausted, she decided to go into the Captain's quarters, where he had a type of fireplace and decided to light it up. Lorraine decided she would stay the night and rest.

Tomorrow she would continue her search for Ron.

THE CREWS

There were ten crews on Crescent, and each crew had between ten to fifty men. Each crew also tried to make as many ships as humanly possible especially since so many would get damaged during the frozen season. The families also had their own family ships which at times they'd live out of instead of their huts on land. The women were usually in charge of the family ships and would occasionally help with the bigger ships that were used to go out to sea.

Crescent was about two hundred miles across, and the island had been split evenly between the crews. The crews kept their ships in the center of the island where the water was not as deep. The women, although worried about their young boys who had to make their seasonal travel to the frozen islands appreciated the custom since it gave them some free time or more time to focus on the younger children. Everyone had to learn basic survival skills such as how to fish and carve spears and what plants were poisonous and so on. There was no crew that was considered better than the other, they had all agreed that each crew would be treated equally as much as possible and whenever a young man became a pirate he was usually assigned to the crew that had the least amount of crew members, there was no guarantee that he could be in the same crew as his father.

QUESTIONS

"Neat," said Shurn" as he gazed down at the frozen waters. Venton had changed himself into the giant bird once again, and he was taking Shurn to the Mythical Valley. He was going to show him the ruins beneath the island from the World before.

"Did you ever hatch any of the eggs" asked Shurn.

"I'd rather not talk about that," said the Wizard. "Why a female bird," asked Shurn' "That's just what I happened to be each time I turned," replied the annoyed Venton. "I have no control over these things," he claimed.

The bird began to cry. He recalled one frozen season when he had to leave the nest to get food; the eggs had been left alone, and when he returned, someone had destroyed his eggs. It was horrible, the shells had been broken, and there was yolk everywhere. They were now about halfway to the mythical valley and below there was a small island. Venton only got to lay eggs every fifty years, and it took at least ten years to hatch them. He had only been successful once. "How do you lay eggs without, you know, a companion" Shurn began to ask...Infuriated Venton screeched loudly, nearly deafening Shurn. "You ask too many needless questions!" said Venton, who now swooped down towards the island and turned causing Shurn to fall off and land on the ground below.

BACK TO THE NEST

Clark had finally decided it was time for him to go back to the nest to look for Brag. Lilly and Leah, two of the bearded women who had become friends with Clark, decided to join him on his trip back. He now had his own pair of furry pants and top in a dark brown color. "This is impressive. What creature are these made of again?" "Black furry camels who used to be abundant in the desert from the World Beneath before the destruction," replied Lilly.

It was hard to imagine what a desert was like for anyone in this constant wintry land. It seemed so otherworldly. "We have some," said Leah. "Really, I'd like to see them," said Clark, but after we find my brothers..."

BAKING

The pie was beginning to smell delicious. There was a knock at the door. Brag opened the door, and it was his three brothers. "Welcome, come in! Come in! So great for you to join me!" Said Brag. Shurn, Clark, and Morven entered the lovely cottage, each carrying a basket. "Oh, you didn't have to," said Brag. "Thank you," he smiled gloriously. "The table is fine," said Brag. The brothers went into the kitchen, savoring the smell of the pie and began to place the baskets on the table. Suddenly, the pie in the oven caught on fire. "Get some water!" yelled Brag, he began to fill a pot with water and throw it in the oven. "Ah!" He yelled as the fire only got worse and began to spread. "Get out! Get out!" He yelled. "Ahhh!" Brag woke up and looked around. He was in a cage. The snow terrors had decided not to eat Brag after all. Instead, they would save him for later.

They were now boiling the large bird eggs they had stolen from Venton and were cooking them in a delicious stew in a large black cauldron. Brag could smell the food from the cage, and it made his stomach grumble.

"Here!" said a snow terror as it slid a plate of food to Brag. "Eat, we can't have you dying on us," it chuckled in an evil tone. Confused, Brag began to eat the food, he had not eaten in so long and decided to risk eating; even if he didn't, he might die from starvation anyway. After a few hours had passed and the terrors had had their fill, they all began to go to sleep. Their bellies were bloated, and they were all so satisfied with the eggs. Brag noticed a key chained around the neck of one of the terrors and was thinking of how he could get it. He began to gather a handful of pebbles from around the cage and was throwing them at the face of the snow terror with the key.

CHAPTER 4

"Welcome," said Master Klink. Venton and Shurn had finally arrived at the Island of the Mythical Valley. "You're a bit early," said the Master. "Yes, yes," said Venton, who was now in human form. Every cold season Venton would fly there to hide from the pirates of the world since it was during that time that the pirates were the most active. "And who is this?" asked Master Klink. "This is Shurn, my new apprentice," said Venton. "I wanted to show him the ruins of the land before," he said. "Of course," ...said the Master. "But first, since you are early join us at the light festival." The light festival was a custom that had begun thousands of years ago before Zidus had blocked out the skies with a fog. Before the curse, the skies in that world had been illuminated by some beautiful lights in the sky that looked like the Aurora Borealis. The lights were best visible during warm weather in the old world.

Now that Zidus had destroyed the land they were no longer seen, but the Montrale Monks had decided to continue their old tradition each year during the time when the lights used to appear.

They hoped that one day they could see them again. The festival was great. There was wonderful music and dancing and a sweet aroma of fresh food all around. There were even games that were played by the local children and the atmosphere, despite its gloom, somehow appeared bright and joyful. Small colorful fires were lit down different pathways, and a local woman (A few women had survived there; she was the first whom Shurn had seen who was not a bearded woman) began to take Shurn on a tour. She told Shurn all about the past that she knew about and showed him some of the different structures that still existed before the downfall. "Here," she said. "What's this" he asked. "Mint ale, it's an ancient recipe that the great knights of the past used to drink," she said.

SERENE

The two had armed up just as Ivene had recommended and were now looking around in amazement.

Whiskers and Xalder were swimming in the Unknown Seas. They noticed some souls that were wandering around and began to swim past them. They held hands as they explored the waters and were extremely alert, fearful of meeting a predator. Whisker's skin had changed to a purple color, and Xalder was now blue. "Where does the monster sleep?" asked Xalder. "I think this way," said Whiskers, who began to lead him away. "Oh" Gasped Whiskers who suddenly stopped and stared to the left near some coral. "That's my sister," she said. Whiskers let go of Xander's hand and swam to a soul that belonged to a long, haired woman. "Come back," he yelled. "No, you don't know what can happen," he called, but it was too late. Whiskers was now trying to hug the soul, but like a ghost, it went right through her, not even noticing her. The ghost's mouth was moving as though trying to speak, but no sound could be heard. It looked as though it was in a zombie-like state with a blank expression and she just kept drifting on without stopping. "Serene, oh Serene" Whiskers began to sob. "It's okay said Xalder and he now hugged Whiskers close to his chest. "That's why we're here, were going to find that key and set her free so she could finally rest," he said.

A LOSS

"Lorraine," said Captain Ron as he gasped looking across the snow. "Lorraine! Lorraine!" he began to shout. The Captain was about to leave to continue his search for the map before the bearded women had captured him until he noticed a figure of a woman in the distance. He recognized her beautiful brown fur. "Ron!" shouted Lorraine as she now began to walk towards him. "Why did you leave Crescent!" He scolded her. "I was worried, and I didn't want to lose you too," she said. "What's all the shouting out here! I'm trying to sleep! Yelled Ivene. Unexpectedly, out of the fog, something huge began to appear from the direction that Lorraine had come. "Molly!" gasped the Captain. "Ahhhh!" He yelled as he now began to pull Lorraine into the cave. "Huh?" mumbled

Ivene confused as she now began to turn and look behind her. "Get in!" shouted Ron, but it was no use, the creature moved too fast and lifted Ivene by her feet, opened its mouth and swallowed Great Mama! "Nooo!" yelled Lorraine and the other bearded women who were now outside the cave trying to see what all the commotion was about. They began to throw rocks and spear the creature and set it on fire, hoping they could kill it before Ivene died inside it. Molly growled and squirted out poisonous black ink as it fought for its life, tossing some of the bearded women yards into the air. One of the bearded women fell on her head and was knocked out unconscious, and another suffered the loss of a limb which was sliced off by one of the creature's claws.

Finally, after what seemed like hours, the creature stopped fighting enough so that they could slice its belly open and pull out Ivene. She was barely alive. "Oh" moaned great Mama as she laid on the ground covered in slimy substance. "Oh "she said as she clenched Lorraine's hand. "I'm glad I got to see you again," said Great Mama. She smiled, touching Lorraine's hand, took one last breath, and died.

What had occurred was Molly had been following Captain Ron's ship and when the ship had frozen in the ice, the creature had just caught up with the ship (By then the pirates had been marched to the cave of the bearded women) and waited until it noticed Lorraine leaving the ship heading to the cave in search of Ron. The octopus had crawled out from the waters and followed Lorraine to the cave from a distance crawling underneath the snow (that is why Lorraine didn't see anything when she'd turn around) and when it noticed Captain Ron it began to charge at him killing Great Mama since she was blocking its path to the Captain.

THE ESCAPE

"What!" grumbled the snow terror as it awoke and now looked at Brag (the terror with the key chained around its neck) Brag then began to make a gesture trying to signal to the creature that he was hungry. "Alright," It mumbled as it began to gather a plate of food for Brag. When he walked over and was about to slide the plate of food to Brag, Brag quickly grabbed the terror's neck and broke it. "That was easy" Thought Brag. The creature's body slipped from his hands and hit the ground with a thud. Another snow terror awoke and looked over at the cage and the terror on the ground; it got up and began to approach Brag, then suddenly a group of snow terrors burst into the room waking up the others shouting, "We've got dinner!" Brag looked across and saw a pirate whom he had never seen tied at his hands and feet trying to get away.

The pirate shrieked making eye contact with Brag with a desperate expression. "Into the pot!" Said a snow terror "Into a pot" They then carried the pirate into another room and Brag could hear the loud, desperate cries of the pirate. The snow terror that had woken up was now fixed on the other pirate in the boiling pot.

Quickly, Brag took the key from the terror's neck and unlocked the door to the cage and got out. He ran towards the entrance trying to ignore the cries from the other pirate feeling awful, but

he knew there was no way he could take them all; there were just too many. Out he ran, and when he made it to the surface, he quickly pushed a large piece of ice that was nearby over the opening of the cave, making sure they couldn't come out. He ran as fast as he could for as long as he could until he was out of breath. He then wept a bit over what he had just seen but continued walking. He was heading to the camp that he and his brothers had set up before Shurn had been taken by the bird.

THE FUTURE

"Shurn," said Venton. "Shurn," he said. Shurn was passed out like a rock on a bed. He had not had such great sleep like that in a while. He had had a bit too much of some mint ale. Shurn grumbled. "It's time to get up," said the wizard. "There is much that I have to show you today, "he said. Shurn sat up and stretched and yawned. When he finally got ready, Shurn's first day of learning had begun.

The wizard then took him to a cave which led him to an underground river beneath a pyramid in the Mythical Valley. As they sailed on a small canoe-like boat down the river, they came to a waterfall that dropped into a vast pit. The two went down, enjoying themselves and once they landed in the water below, Venton told Shurn to follow him as he dived in. Under the water, they could see clearly, and Shurn could see old ruins from what appeared to be an ancient building.

CHAPTER 5

Time had passed, and the frozen season was nearing its end.

Whiskers and Xalder had found the key. A giant sea creature had swallowed them while they were mermaids and found the key in its belly. They were able to safely get out of the creature, although, while they had been trapped inside it (The creature was about fifty feet wide) they had absorbed some of the creature's bodily fluids which caused them to experience strange hallucinations. At one-point Whiskers had to smack Xalder. He thought she had been a talking apple pie asking him to bite her. Despite that, they kept their sanity and were able to return to the cave of the bearded women right when the spell wore off. When they arrived, they were deeply saddened by the loss of Great Mama, and they held a traditional bearded woman funeral for her.

They dressed Ivene in her favorite outfit and wrapped her body in a warm perfumed blanket and set her on a sled that they then set on fire and spread her ashes throughout the land.

Clark, with Leah and Lilly, eventually found Brag (he had been found wandering around lost) and brought him back to the cave of the Bearded women. Captain Ron and Lorraine had never gone to seek the map after all; instead, they decided to stay until the cold season arrived. Lorraine needed to cope over the loss of Ivene. Ivene had been like a mother to her, and Lorraine felt guilty for not coming to see her sooner. The map had been found by Shurn in the ruins beneath the Island of the Mythical Valley.

The bearded women hunted down the dwelling of the Snow Terrors and destroyed their home, and they turned the captives into new furry clothes. Venton had found the cave of the bearded women and told them about the Island of the Mythical Valley. He had apologized for taking Shurn and told Shurn's brothers his plans of making Shurn the new Necromancer for generations to come. Shurn was beginning to learn magic. The pirates of Crescent were now beginning to set things up for the young boys who would soon return home from the Frozen Islands. Each year when the adolescent pirates returned home, their parents would hold a great feast congratulating the boys for being so mature and independent.

The parents were always so proud and gave them gifts. The gifts consisted of necklaces or new boots, and so forth. The Wizard Venton was now on his way to Crescent, he was trying to gather everyone together, so they could make plans on how to destroy or lock Zidus up once again and restore the World to its earlier form. Now that Shurn had the map, Master Klink and a crew were on their way to retrieve it.

THE WINDS

The winds began to change, as they did each year showing that the Frozen season had ended.

Instead of them blowing east into Crescent they now blew west, which would soon help the pirates in their time of sail when it was almost time for the ships to go exploring and fishing. The fog was dimming a bit, sadly there was still no sun, but the sky would be light grey instead of dark grey, and different creatures would soon begin to appear.

The strange murmur could now be heard too. No one knew what the murmur was, but it was soft and constant and could be heard coming from below the waters. Some pirates believed it was the sound of the souls, while others claimed it was the heartbeat of Zidus.

DRAGON BLOOD

"He's going to make you drink dragon blood," said Master Klink. The Master and the future wizard (Shurn) along with a crew from the Mythical Valley were abroad the Betty. The Master had named his great ship the Betty because he just thought it was catchy. She was a vast boat which could hold up to four hundred men, and it was made from the wood of the white pines of the Mythical Valley. The trees were literally white and looked beautiful. "Why do I have to drink dragon blood," asked the Wizard Shurn. "It's going to transform you. You *really* shouldn't complain; it is a privilege that many people would kill for," replied Master Klink. "What will happen when I drink this" asked Shurn. "I don't know; the gift is different for everyone. Some wizards become taller, others their eyes change, some become immune to allergies...but one thing is for certain, your magic will become more powerful," said the Master. "I'm intrigued," said Shurn. "Master!" someone shouted, "Master!" A hole! We're heading to a hole; we must turn!" The crew was beginning to be sucked into a hole, the ship was beginning to lean, and strong winds like a giant tornado were starting to blow. Sea creatures were being blown threw the air, and lightning was beginning to strike. The crew were frantic and trying their best to control the ship and direct it away from the hole. "Get it off! Get it off!" yelled one of the pirates. A shark landed on top of one of the crew members and began to bite him. "Ahhh," he yelled as his arm was devoured. The crew took some long spears and pushed the creature back into the sea. The mangled pirate just sat in shock, clenching his arm while another was trying to keep him from bleeding out. "Shurn!" yelled the Master. "Shurn do something," he screamed. Shurn began to say something in a strange language that sounded like a dialect of French and Arabic then he clapped his hands together, and he began to blow the sails away from the hole.

THE DEVIL

"It's the bird!" Yelled a pirate. Venton had finally arrived at Crescent and tried to land until a spear was thrown at him. He screeched and then landed on a tree. Poof! He became human. "Stop!" he bellowed. Everyone now stared up in awe at him, for they had never seen a wizard before. The pirates of Crescent had only heard myths and legends about wizards before the curse. "It's the devil!" yelled another pirate. Suddenly, all the people in the village began to run and scream and hide in their homes. "Oh, dear" mumbled the wizard. "I swear to you, I am not the devil!" yelled Venton. "Prove it!" said someone. "Prove that you're not the devil!" "How," he asked. "Eat this," said a lady as she threw a green potato looking vegetable at him.

"What is it," asked the wizard. "It's meshi. If you're not the devil, then you shouldn't die when you eat this." Venton looked at the vegetable and then after hesitating a bit he bit into the disgusting thing and swallowed it. "Uh!" He tried not to hurl. "He's not the devil," said a child. "He's still alive!" "Well, who are you then," asked a person. "I am Venton" I have come to seek your help," he began to explain.

CLARK AND LILLY

"This is so lovely," said Lilly as she now gave Clark a long romantic kiss. "You are the most beautiful woman I have ever seen," said Clark. Lilly blushed. Clark had taken Lilly to the location where the brothers had left their ship. The two love birds had made camp and were gathering material to repair the ship, so it could sail once again. Lilly wanted to leave the cave of the bearded women and go traveling to all the interesting places that Clark had told her about. They had become quite a happy couple. "It's time for dinner," said Clark, they had set up a fire near the ship and were now eating. "Tomorrow we'll begin the repairs," said Clark.

GREAT ENCHANTER

"My arm" cried the pirate who had been bitten by a shark. "My arm," he cried. The crew had survived. Shurn had created a wind that sailed the ship away from the hole, and they were now back on track. "Impressive!" Said Master Klink looking at Shurn. "Look there!" exclaimed a pirate. "Were here!" he said. After about an hour, the pirates arrived onshore. They split into two groups and began to explore the land in search of the necklace. The pirate who had lost his arm stayed behind with one of the crew members who was treating him. Back on Crescent, Venton had finally gotten the pirates to join in destroying Zidus.

One of the crews was on its way to the cave of the bearded women. They planned to pick them up, so they could join in on the capture of Zidus. The other ships were headed out to sea to the location where Zidus was most likely seen, and one crew stayed behind in case the boys on the Frozen Islands returned before Zidus was captured. Venton was now flying back to get the dragon blood which he had kept hidden all this time. He needed to take it to Shurn soon for he was dying. What had happened, when Venton had turned himself into a human after abducting Shurn, his life was beginning to run out sooner since he had stayed alive unnaturally. He needed to quickly choose an apprentice, or there would be no one left with magic after he died.

GATHERED GROUP

After a few days, everyone was now ready. All the ships were anxiously waiting. As soon as the Betty arrived, it would be time, and although they knew not everyone would survive, no one backed out. Xalder and Whiskers were sitting together, holding the key. They still had the jar of potion that had transformed them into mermaids, when the creature arrived to the surface, Xalder (because he was the chosen one) was going to be the one to put the necklace on the creature and lure him into the cave while Whiskers and Shurn would wait for him to get out and they would both lock the door while Shurn was going to hold him back. "There!" said Captain Ron as he pointed. Master Klink is here. "Shurn come!' Shouted Venton. Shurn approached the Great Wizard, who had now grown weak. Venton was not going to take part since this was going to be his last lesson for Shurn. Venton would not aid him in any way. "It was a pleasure to be your teacher," said Venton proudly. "You will all be left in great hands; my apprentice has been taught well and has proven himself worthy," he said. All pirates began to cheer and congratulate Shurn. "Thank you," said Shurn as he bowed humbly. Venton now handed Shurn a small tube with dragon blood and smiled. "You may drink it now," said Venton.

DRAGON BLOOD

Shurn drank the dragon blood, and then suddenly he changed. His eyes turned white, and his veins protruded a bit. He aged as well, and now his hair was grey and long, and he had a beard. He looked much wiser than before and had a glow to his complexion. "I must go now," said Venton. "I haven't much time left, and I don't want to spend the rest of my life out here," said Venton. Shurn hugged Venton, and then the dying wizard turned into a bird and flew away.

"It is time!" said the new Necromancer.

The Betty had finally arrived, and now they began to summon the creature. The pirates began to toss some rocks into the ocean and shouted as loud as they could trying to lure it up. After a few moments, the ships began to creak, and waves were beginning to rise, and rain began to fall. "Everyone get ready!" yelled Shurn. "There!" yelled a pirate pointing at the water. The beast had poked its gigantic head out of the water and gawked at the ships with its fierce red eyes that were larger than a pirate then went below the waters again. "Where'd it go!" Said another pirate. Suddenly the waves stopped, and a flock of birds began to come down onto the ships. 'Ahhh they yelled as the birds came down hitting their heads and squawking.

"Suddenly, the waves began again, and the skies grew black. They were blacker than they had ever been any time before. "Ahhh!" yelled a pirate. The creature had come back up directly under one of the ships and flung it into the sky.

"Attack!" yelled Shurn. "Attack!"

The ships were now blowing cannons at the monster barely scratching it. The pirates that had been flung into the air were now trying to swim onto the other ships trying to stay alive. Captain Ron pushed a pirate out of his way and loaded a cannon.

He fired it, hitting the beast right in the eye. "The monster roared deafening the pirates as it tossed its head in pain. "Keep firing!" yelled Master Klink. The monster then began to swim to the ship that Ron was on and went under. "Abandon ship!" Abandon ship! It was too late. The ship was tossed into the air like a rag doll and came crashing down into the waters. "Here!" yelled Xalder. "Here!" he tried to pull the Captain out of the water, but it was no use. A giant tentacle came up and grabbed the Captain pulling him down. Xalder then drank the potion (the potion Ivene had given him) and jumped in; Whiskers went down after Xalder. "The Key!" yelled a pirate. "They forgot the key!"

THE DOOR

Shurn grabbed the key and jumped into the water. He swam as fast as he could. He could see the creature moving quickly below. The beast was taking Ron to its cave, and Xalder was now on its neck, struggling to get the necklace on it. Whiskers was crawling up the creature from its tail. Suddenly, Shurn changed into a shark and began to swim after them. "Take the key!" he said to Whiskers, who nearly died of fear when she saw him." "It's me, take the key," said Shurn. Whiskers grabbed the key with one hand while still holding on to the beast's tail, then Shurn swam up and bit the tentacle which was holding Ron. The creature moaned and tossed the Captain but then continued swimming. Shurn lifted the Captain in his mouth and took him to the surface. Xalder finally turned into a mermaid and then dropped the potion (there was still some potion in the jar). He looked at Whiskers, and when she made eye contact, he pointed at the potion on the ground. Whiskers understood and then she went after the potion and drank it. Finally, Xalder got the necklace around the creature. The creature then began to swim up to the surface again towards the ships. "Where's the door" asked Xalder. The two mermaids then began to search for the door.

AGAIN

"They put the necklace on it!" yelled a pirate. Shurn was now a human again. Captain Ron had been placed inside his quarters when he reached the surface. He had a deep wound, but he was fine." "Oh good," they put the necklace on him. Said Ron. Shurn lifted his hands and began to speak in the strange enchanter language. His voice boomed and echoed, and his eyes began to glow as lightning now began to strike.

The creature came up again out of the water and began to toss some of the pirates into the air. As Shurn continued speaking (he was casting a spell for the necklace to control it) the creature began to twist and beat its monstrous arms against the waters, but it was no use. Shurn was in control of the creature now, and he ordered it back into the seas. Zidus obeyed, and he began to head to the door beneath the waters where it had been trapped before. Whiskers and Xalder had found the door and opened it. As they were about to swim back to the surface, they saw the creature heading towards them. Whiskers clenched Xalders hand as the creature went inside its cave. The two mermaids shut the door and locked it. Zidus let out a loud monstrous cry.

THE CURSE IS GONE

The curse was now gone. The massive storm stopped, and the fog began to disappear. The pirates cheered. The souls that had been trapped by Zidus rose from the waters and went up into the heavens above. They were now at peace. The Captain recognized Romus and waved him goodbye one last time. "Thank you, father," said Romus as he disappeared into the clouds.

It was a bittersweet victory. Not all had made it, but their deaths were not in vain. The pirates began to gather the bodies of the ones that had died and loaded them onto the ships. When that was complete, they all began to head back to Crescent. Xalder and Whiskers swam behind until the mermaid spell wore off.

"What is that?" asked a young boy who was pointing at the moon. The young boys from the Frozen Islands had just arrived home.

Many of them saddened by the loss of their fathers. The moon from the world before began to show again as they had in the past. The four seasons from before had returned, and the waters had subsided showing the land from before. Plants that had gone extinct were beginning to bloom again, and people were enjoying sunshine again.

Xalder and Whiskers stayed on Crescent and had a family. Lilly and Clark completed repairing the old ship that his brothers used to explore in. (Clark named the ship Lilly) They eventually had children and lived out their dreams exploring the great new world. Brag decided to stay at the cave with the bearded women and would occasionally visit Crescent. Eventually, he fell in love and went on to have children. Shurn continued to study magic and eventually opened a school on Crescent. Magic was now a requirement for young pirates. Finally, Venton lived out the rest of his days on the Mythical Valley, embracing the wonderful festivals that commonly happened, but there were also rumors that he had been laying more eggs...

Rebecka Lynn is an American Author who enjoys drafting books for young children (many which rhyme) and humorous fantasy/adventure books for teens and young adults. As a child, Rebecka was known to have a vivid imagination and enjoyed reading books by Edgar Allen Poe and C.S. Lewis. Rebecka's first book is The Petrified Kingdom of the Gourges which; was first, thought of in 2014 and published in 2018.

To my Readers,

Thank you for making it to the end of my book. I hope that you enjoyed it. If you did, more are at:

amazon.com/author/lillydlynn

Made in the USA
Columbia, SC
02 September 2020